Donald So

I, MEAH

Onwards and Upwards Publishers

Onwards and Upwards Publications
Berkeley House
11 Nightingale Crescent
West Horsley
Surrey
KT24 6PD
England

www.onwardsandupwards.org

This edition published 2011

copyright © Donald Southey

The right of Donald Southey to be identified as the author of this work has been asserted by him in accordance with the Copyright, Designs and Patents Act 1988.

All rights reserved.

No part of this publication may be reproduced or transmitted in any form or by any means, electronic or mechanical, including photocopy, recording or any information storage and retrieval system, without permission in writing from the author or publisher.

ISBN: 978-1-907509-09-4

Cover design: Leah-Maarit

Printed in the UK

The Three Laws of Robotics
(paraphrased from Isaac Asimov)

<u>First Law</u>: A robot shall never cause any harm to a human being; nor, by his inaction, endanger or allow harm to come to a human being.

<u>Second Law:</u> Subject to the First Law, a robot shall obey every direct command of a human being; firstly of his master, then of any other human.

<u>Third Law:</u> Subject to the First and Second Laws, a robot shall always endeavour to preserve his own safety and that of other robots.

ACKNOWLEDGEMENTS

Nearly every author who has written about robots in the last fifty years owes some debt of inspiration to Isaac Asimov, and I for one am happy to acknowledge mine. One of the central questions explored in my novel I first encountered about forty years ago in a short story that was probably <u>not</u> by Asimov, and which I have been unable to trace since; to that unknown author, I also wish to record my gratitude.

And I must not fail to mention my daughters, all of whom have said at some point, "Dad, we really ought to get you published." My wife, for believing in me; the many members of Freedom Church who encouraged me; Mark and Diana at Onwards And Upwards Publishers; and Robin, the ex-missionary and bookshop manager, who finally tipped the scales, singling out this story and saying, "You MUST publish Sid."

FOREWORD

.........Not sure quite what to expect, I enthusiastically began to read. From the word go all other activities planned for my morning were curtailed, as I found myself happily lost, yet somehow at home with the scenario unfolding as I read on. In the beginning, the descriptive writing suggested to me this book may be biased toward those who love attention to detail, maybe at the expense of a riveting plot, but any fears I had were quickly dispersed as I became endeared to a man, a robot, and a touching relationship developing between the two. This book made me ask myself, 'What If?'.... A picture of a future life living with a personal robot! ..

This is a story of the power of the soul, and how awful life would be without it....... A picture of our current humanity where raw honesty, trust and purity of heart are sorely missing. This threw me a challenge to stand up for my beliefs, and consider my own role of following a way of life, however hard, to the very best end. However simple, one selfless deed done reflecting the heart of love, can change someone forever. Read on, and allow yourself time to enjoy, to be moved, and, ultimately enlightened.

Chris Eaton, singer/songwriter/producer/believer.

Donald Southey

I never used to believe in God.

In fact, I probably still wouldn't, if it hadn't been for Sid, my robot.

You've obviously heard of the phenomenon. If you know a bit more than most people about it, you'll be saying, "What, *that* Sid?"

And you'd be right. And that also tells you why I'm writing this anonymously.

No-one knows yet just what to make of Sid, nor of his legacy. The government, of course, doesn't like it. But they still haven't moved to stop it. They're just watching, very, very carefully.

I ordered Sid just two years ago. It seems like half a lifetime.

'Davy' Jones made him; it was before he became famous, never mind notorious.

Davy wasn't his real name, just a nickname that everybody used, from his colleagues at Warwick University to his mates at that big church he attended. I always thought that anyone who went to a church would be a head-in-the-sand type, never a scientist, which just shows how wrong you can be.

Warwick was then, as now, one of the top five centres of excellence in cybernetic research and advanced robotics in the world, right up there with MIT, Kyoto, Seoul and Dresden. Davy Jones was a recent Ph.D. who had just accepted a professorship there. However, he had funded his studies by customizing robots for people, and still had a waiting list. I think mine was the last order he accepted before becoming a mainstream lecturer.

What he was offering was the most advanced robotic brain available on the market. He held the patents, and he and his lab team understood the technologies better than anyone else. They were a full three years ahead of the Japanese, and that was amazing, when you considered the price. It meant that at a stretch, and/or a hefty loan, an ordinary professional like me could get bleeding edge technology for a home robot.

He needed the money, I wanted the robot, the lab staff got overtime, the university officially didn't know but unofficially got some research expenses met, everyone was happy.

Sid was a standard Series Five robot before he was customized. I had made a windfall earlier that year by leaving one job with a golden handshake, and walking into another with a golden hello. I was flush and feeling a little reckless. But unlike some, I didn't take early retirement (much too long to go), or cruise round the world (hate the idea of cruises), or backpack across Nepal (too much like hard work), or head for Las Vegas (not quite that stupid). I treated myself to the best robot I could buy. I had the full anthropomorphic package put on him – it was always going to be a 'him', I didn't want a Cherry-2000 cyber-mistress – and booked a custom brain from Warwick's website. The blurb said that it made a robot into a companion, and that was what I needed, after my divorce.

Sid was officially described as a Self Instructing Decision Making Intelligent Cyber-Servant, version 3; but SIDMICS-3 was such a crap name, that I called him Sid for short, and it stuck. (You always wondered what sort of a dumb name Sid was, didn't you? Now you know how he got it.)

I met Davy Jones the week after I ordered the brain. I think he wanted to suss me out, see whether I was really up for trying out something hot from the lab, or whether I might sue him if it didn't quite meet expectations.

"I don't mind being a bit of a beta-test-site," I said. "I've got a little money to burn; obviously I don't want to waste it, but if it doesn't quite work out – well, not the end of the world. I'll still have a home robot that is at least as good as anything I can get elsewhere, won't I?"

"Oh yes," said Davy earnestly. "We're 99% sure it will actually be way in advance of anything you'll get in the next five years. And we do give a warranty – if it fails in service within two years, we'll repair it, or if we can't, we'll replace with a standard, manufacturer's brain and refund you the full difference."

"That's a verifiable functional failure as opposed to one of the advanced mental capabilities?"

"Well, yes." His brow was a little furrowed. "Not that we expect …"

"OK. I'm cool with that."

His face lit up. "You are? Great."

I then asked a silly question.

"I've read the website description, but – can you walk me through the differences between your advanced model and the usual ones that I can buy off the shelf?"

Cue an hour's fascinating demo and lecture in the laboratory.

"You'll remember the Series One robots, I expect."

Davy was busily cleaning dry marker off a printing-whiteboard.

"Yes, I remember – total morons, by today's standards."

"Right, absolutely right. The difference is all in the brain, of course. The general mechatronics have only advanced by a factor of two – in complexity and in miniaturization. The brain is another matter altogether." He started drawing vigorously on the whiteboard.

"All robot brains follow the same general principle, established twenty years ago. Essentially, they imitate the human brain, with very simple units – neurons – highly interconnected. Here's a sketch of the brain of the Series One. It's made up of a whole array of little cubes, like this. Each one has six faces, and –"

"Hold on," I interrupted. "What's in the cubes?"

"A neuron equivalent in silicon – a minicontroller, basically. RISC microprocessor, tiny bit of read-only memory for the basic instructions and boot-up, some input-output buffering, fuzzy logic, adaptive voting module, master control serial bus, and a bit of read-write memory."

"Remind me … RISC?"

"Reduced Instruction Set Computer – does a very few things very fast."

"Sounds like a lot more than a neuron."

"It has to be. Even with micro-technology, we are still working at a level far below the complexity of any mammalian brain. We just can't put it together on a big enough scale yet."

"What's the limitation?"

"There are several. The first one is the sheer time it takes to assemble 10 billion pieces into a system, connecting and testing as you go. Can't be done – we have to call it a day at around 50 million. The next one is interconnectivity – the human brain beats anything we can do by a couple of orders of magnitude." He took off his glasses and polished them. "Those are the main two."

"OK … so you have a few million little cubes and you interconnect them."

"Yes, and this is where it gets interesting," he said, his eyes lighting up again behind his glasses. He rapidly finished his sketch.

"The Mark One brain was a simple arrangement of cubic processors," he said, pointing to one. "If you put cubes in an orthogonal array … sorry … if you just line them all up, in rows and columns, you get six faces touching. You need three faces for power, ground, and the master serial bus, so you only have three left for interconnection. Useless."

"Did the Series One robots have a brain arranged like that?"

"No. Mark One had alternate rows offset, by half a cube, in two dimensions. That meant that every cube is touching" – he stabbed with his finger, counting them off – "six, plus two this side, two that side, ten in all; three reserved, so seven degrees of interconnection. It was just enough."

"Almost like a brick wall, but many bricks deep."

"Yes, almost. Actually, they tried traditional brick wall patterns, or weaves - all kinds of arrangements – but most gave no advantage, and others required too many different sizes of brick, and so on. The only way they could improve it was to rethink the whole morphology."

"Couldn't they interconnect at the corners or something?"

"Ah! Yes, we're coming to that. But that was a last resort – we are talking nanotechnology here, a corner is not something you want to spot-weld a wire to, not at this sort of size … So Mark Two took a different basic shape as its starting point." He was scribbling again.

"Here we are; the honeycomb. Nearly the best possible ratio of surface-area to contained volume, AND you can get to all the cells – an amazing combination. Each cell is touching six others around it, and three at the end. And the front face? Because it's so accessible, it can carry power, ground, *and* the serial bus, all attached to the one surface. That still leaves nine for interconnection."

"That was the Mark Two? What was the Mark Three then?"

"The Mark Three still used the honeycomb, but put the layers together differently. This was where the team here had got to when I joined. They had developed a technique of layering the power, ground and bus to snake through the honeycomb, each borrowing only half a wall of each cell, and freeing up the end wall. This could now become like the other end, touching the next layer with a three-way connection. Result: twelve degrees of interconnection."

"Was that why the Series Three robots were such a huge improvement?"

"Absolutely. The thing is, just adding one degree of interconnection gives something like half an order of magnitude in capability. We added *three*. The Mark Three robots were the first to be self-teaching; they were pre-programmed with the Laws, of course, and a lot of other basics, and learned everything else as they went. They were the first truly adaptive robots, and the first to be used in high-trust and safety-critical situations."

"And now you're on to Series Five."

"Yes. This was my doctorate study." He grinned. "You can't buy 'em in the shops, yet."

"Only from the University."

"Indeed. Well, I said that the honeycomb was nearly the most efficient packaging you can get – meet the most efficient of all. It's called" – he caught my eye – "ah, a long Greek name, but it's a fourteen-sided 3-D shape, and it nests perfectly. Best thing is, it touches fourteen of its neighbours."

"So you get fourteen degrees of interconnection?"

"Not on its own. You still need to get the power, ground and serial bus in somewhere. That's not as easy as with the hexagons. But," he grinned, "with the aid of a small mainframe computer, we got *more* than fourteen."

"How?"

"My little contribution – the plane surfaces, on all these shapes, are metalled, and interconnect with each other. You always leave the vertices – the points – and the edges un-metalled, to stop things shorting out. I left an un-metalled border on each face and metalled half the edges."

"How many interconnects did that give you?"

"Depends how you use them. At first, we just used four, for power, ground, serial bus, and one extra interconnect- fifteen degrees of interconnection. That was the Mark Four." He paused and wiped his glasses again. "The Series Four robots are fully autonomous. They are programmed with the Three Laws, and can make judgment calls in situations of potential decision conflict. They can steer their own learning. One of them went to a man who smoked. The robot found out, all by itself, that smoking is harmful, and most courteously requested him to stop – every time he lit up."

"What – the robot even worked out how to ask him politely?"

"Yes. I had to deal with it myself. They can all hold an intelligent conversation, none of it pre-programmed except the English language itself. They appear to be able to conceptualize. If you think about what they can teach themselves to do, it's quite staggering."

"And the Mark Five?"

"Up to this month, we've used six edge connections- seventeen degrees of interconnection. They have all the capabilities of the Mark Four, and then some. We've actually run ahead of our ability to pre-programme them. Their learning ability is awesome. They can repair their own memories – one was in an accident, and part of its brain was fried, but it recovered 100% inside a week. They can handle philosophical concepts." He looked me in the eye. "Don't laugh. We estimate they are two orders of magnitude below the human brain in complexity, in roughly twice the space, and we haven't mapped the full extent of what they can do yet."

"They're safe, I hope?"

"Oh yes – the Inspectorate has given them the highest rating yet. There are about a hundred in use so far. We're about to go into full batch production. It was the spec. for these you saw on the website. Yours, though, will be a little different from the rest."

"How's that?"

"The configuration uses eight edge connections, nineteen degrees of interconnection. If you're up for it, we think this is where it's going to get really interesting."

What an understatement.

Sid was delivered, minus brain, direct to Warwick. Mitsubishi kindly invited me to inspect him before I paid the bill. How does one inspect a robot with no brain? One of Davy Jones' assistants wired him up to a test rig and we saw all his limbs and segments move. There were no fluid leaks, no grommets missing from cable holes. The prosthetics looked good. I signed.

Eight weeks later, I had a card through my door informing me that a 'package, other', that would not fit through my letterbox, and needed my signature, awaited me at the sorting office.

When I got there, late that afternoon, the clerk passed the receipt through the hatch for me to sign, and went to fetch the 'package, other'. When I looked up from signing, a face I did not immediately recognize met my gaze. A hand extended gracefully through the hatch. Only as I took it, and felt its inhuman coolness, did the truth hit me like an electric shock.

Donald Southey

"Hello, Mr. Smith," said the apparent human. (He used my real name, of course.) "I'm most glad to meet you. I recognise you because I have seen your photograph. I am told your name for me was Sid. Is that still correct?"

"Hello, Sid," I gulped. "Yes, that's fine. The name, I mean. Glad to meet you too."

I was panicking because I was doing this all wrong. Robots don't understand bad grammar, topic jumps, implied subjects. I drew breath.

"Your name is Sid. I gave you that name …"

"That's fine," interrupted the robot with a smile. Interrupted? Robots never interrupt. "Shall we go home? I will be most interested to see your home."

The whole experience was staggering from the very start. It wasn't *like* talking to a robot. It was more like talking to a foreigner with a good command of English. Intonation, inflection, emphasis – they were all there; not perfect, but like a human's second language. If you were talking to him over the phone, it would have taken you quite a while to tumble to the truth.

The particular thing I still remember fixing on in amazement at the time was the fluidity and naturalness of Sid's movements. He had never been in this building before – he had never been in this town before – but he unlatched the office door, turned to call his thanks to the clerk, picked up his sports bag, shut the door behind him, stepped around me to open the outer door, and walked with me down the steps with the grace of a dancer.

He was *good*, no doubt about it. Most robots I had ever encountered – up to that point – would have needed three attempts just to get down the steps; preferably with an instructor.

With no prompting, he followed me, without stepping on my heels, and even walking around to the other side of my car as I stopped to unlock it. The pre-programming was fantastic.

We got home; I showed him the rooms; I showed him the recharge point and the maintenance kit in the garage. I assumed he was capable of routine self-maintenance.

"Do you need instruction in any of these procedures?"

"Oh, no, thank you. I have been instructed in reading, and in the use of tools. Do you have the manuals?"

He's going to read his own manuals?

I didn't argue. I found them for him.

"Thank you. Shall I prepare a meal for you?"

"Uh … no, thanks, that's okay …" I was doing it again. "I mean, that won't be necessary. I usually fix my own meals."

"In that case, might I watch you when you do so? It would be very instructive for me."

"Really…?"

"Yes. It is my duty to understand all your

preferences, and as much about your lifestyle as I can. It helps me to serve you with intelligence."

I was already feeling exhausted. I raided the freezer for pizza.

Not only did Sid watch me, he engaged me in conversation.

"Do you enjoy frozen ready meals, Mr. Smith?"

"They're not my favourite ... I'm just getting this one because I'm tired, and I don't want the work of cooking something from scratch."

I was making excuses for my behaviour to a robot. Was I mad, or was it just because he was so *human?*

"By the way, call me John – in the house, anyway."

"Very well, John," said Sid, slipping into it without a trace of hesitation. "Shall I call you John at other times when we are alone?"

This was doing my head in. A robot making suggestions, about a hypothetical situation ...

"Yes, all right," I replied, a little irritably. Did he know how to read our emotions? It seemed that he did. "I'm sorry if I asked a wrong question, John."

"No ... you didn't. It was a very intelligent question, actually. I'm just a bit tired."

"Am I talking too much?"

A considerate robot, now. "Maybe a little. This is all new to me too, you know."

"Of course, John, I'll just keep quiet for a little while and observe. Is that okay?"

"Yes, that's okay."

The next curious thing happened at bedtime. Sid almost begged to be allowed to wash up. I had shown him where the plates and things went, and kept an eye on him while he finished that and did some other simple chores. Then I told him his duties were finished for the day.

"While you are in your bedroom, John, is it correct that I only enter if you call me?"

"Yes, that's correct ... unless there is an emergency, of course. A house fire, for instance."

"Of course, and if I need you for any reason, may I knock on the door and wait?"

This surprised me, but I supposed he was programmed to ask. "Yes, do that."

I showed him out to the garage, gave him the key to the interconnecting door, and checked that his charger was working properly.

"I shall relax for a bit in the lounge, before I go to bed. See you in the morning."

"Thank you for everything. Goodnight."

"Goodnight."

I had settled down in front of the TV when I heard noises from the garage. I got up to see what the matter was, and met Sid coming through the kitchen.

"I'm very sorry to disturb you, John, but may I ask a favour?"

"Er... yes, I suppose so."

"May I have a couch, or a reclining chair, in my room? My recharging does not work fully if I have to stand and balance. If I could recline, it would be much better for me."

I had a reclining armchair that I didn't use much, but it wouldn't go through the garage door.

"I think," I said after a few abortive attempts, "that we'd better bring your charger into the house instead."

I settled him into the recliner in the dining room. I left him plugged in, with a blissful smile on his face and his eyes shut.

The following morning I phoned Davy Jones.

"He *sleeps!*" I told him. "I've never heard of a robot that sleeps. Did you expect that?"

There was a stunned silence on the other end. "Davy?"

"Yes … yes, I'm still here … No, I had no idea."

"Did he not sleep while he was with you?"

"Well, we always lie them down to recharge in the lab, but that's purely a safety precaution. I tested him recharging standing up, once at least – we always do that …"

"But you never saw him sleeping?"

"I don't know … I wasn't looking for that. Wait a moment."

He came back to the phone after a few moments.

"Sean, my lab assistant, says Sid often recharged with his eyes shut. His brain was still showing activity, but at a lower level, on average. We presumed it was a feature of the extra connectivity. While he wasn't learning, some of his brain could idle, as it were."

"Well, he definitely slept last night. I walked through the room where he was recharging, and he never stirred."

"That's extraordinary ... Look, could we have him back here for a few days or nights?"

Sid was clearly disappointed to be going back.

"I'm so sorry if I have not given you satisfaction, John," he said. "I have only been with you one day, and I know I have much to learn."

"Sid, I'm not sending you back – not permanently," I explained. "Mr. Davy Jones wants to have you back for a few days, maybe a week, for some more tests. You ... well, you're a very unusual robot, and we are all learning about *you*, too."

"If I perform satisfactorily in the tests, will I be able to come back to live with you?"

To live with me. Yes, it was already like having another living person in the house.

"Oh yes. I mean, as far as I can see, that will be no problem."

"I should like that very much."

How can a robot experience pleasure and pain? I put it down to a complex reaction to his experiences versus the Laws and his advanced programming that imitated emotion.

"Don't worry, Sid. I'm sure that you will do fine."

"You have confidence in me?" His face brightened.

"Yes, I have every confidence in you, Sid."

Sid stayed at Warwick, that time, for nine days.

Davy Jones confirmed that Sid did indeed 'sleep', or something very like it. He also confirmed that Sid always awoke instantly if he detected any danger, so there was no safety issue. Like most advanced robots, he could detect smoke, motion, an electrical short before it became a fire, all kinds of things, and could filter usual house noises from unexpected ones.

"Did you find out why he sleeps?"

"Not entirely. He seems to need it to maintain his brainpower. From Day 3, we put him on a regime of recharging while interacting with humans. We found a distinct slowdown in his learning ability, and after forty-eight hours he was really losing it … just like human fatigue, really. We let him lie down and recharge without distraction for eight hours, and he was fine again. I can only surmise it's a function of his complexity."

"I hope he hasn't gone off me, putting him through that."

"You'll be fine with him," said Davy. "He's anxious to please without being obsessive – we got the balance pretty well there – and from what you say, a projective learner, just as we hoped."

"I'm impressed with his language skills … How did you do that?"

"Ah." He tapped his nose. "We played him videos before you got him. Non-stop, every day for three weeks, after initial programming. Like a total-immersion course in language and culture."

"Well, he's amazing. It really is like having another human around."

Davy grinned. "So you'll keep him, for now?"

"Yeah. For now."

Sid and I got on famously for the next few weeks. Every day there was some slight refinement in his speech, his behaviours, his humanness. At times I had to pinch myself to make sure I wasn't imagining I was talking with a human friend, a friend who had an endless capacity for chores and conversation.

He was learning colossal amounts. About twice a week I had to take him to the library to exchange books, usually up to my limit of six at a time. He got all the language courses out, one by one, and added a new tongue to his repertoire about once a fortnight. He didn't need as much sleep as me – about five hours a night did him fine – and if I left my bedroom door open I could distantly hear him practicing French verbs, or Chinese tones, past midnight.

His motor skills and non-academic learning were coming on in leaps and bounds, too. One day I showed him how to use a paintbrush, and by the end of the weekend he had repainted every doorframe, skirting board, and other piece of wood in the house – immaculately.

One thing I kept him away from was the television. Davy Jones had suggested that news and talk shows might confuse him in the early days, and I wasn't inclined to take the risk yet.

But I didn't forbid him to watch it; in fact I simply didn't mention it, and one day I came in to find him wide-eyed in front of the news. There had been a nasty suicide bombing somewhere in Palestine, I think.

He turned to me. "Is this true?" he asked in appalled tones.

I could have lied to him, I suppose, but he would have found out sooner or later.

"Yes," I said. "It's basically true. A little is opinion, but most of it is true."

He turned to look at the screen again. He shook his head slowly. "I cannot comprehend it."

I had no idea how to handle this. "Do you want to go and talk to Mr. Davy Jones about it?"

He shook his head again, without taking his eyes from the screen. "You are my friend. I would rather talk with you, John, if that's okay."

"OK."

We sat in silence for the remainder of the newscast. It ended, as always, with who had thrashed who in the football.

Finally he turned to me. "Is this all true?"

"Most of it is true," I replied. "Like I said, some

is speculation, but most is true. You won't get all the truth from that broadcast, you understand, some will come out later …"

"I have heard that sometimes, men forget the First Law, and harm each other. But this … I had no idea. You live in such violent times."

"Well, I'm sorry to say that we're used to it. In fact, it's really not as bad as it has been, even in my memory."

"You astound me." Sid gestured towards the television – just like a human. "Here in our country, cities are fighting each other. Newcastle has just been victorious over Birmingham …"

I laughed, which confused him even more. "That's not war, its football. It's a game, a sport, a test between friendly rivals."

"But I saw the fighting in the street. The police were hardly able to stop it spreading."

I stopped chuckling. "Oh, that. Well … some people, a very few, want to take it too far."

That was Sid's introduction to another side of human behaviour. I phoned Davy and told him what had happened. He apologised profoundly.

"You think you've covered all the important bases, and then something like this comes out of left field … no pun intended … I'm really sorry. You both okay now?"

I, MESSIAH

I ended up taking Sid to a football match on the following Saturday. He was goggle-eyed, taking it all in.

He asked endless questions afterwards, and I was beginning to fear he might try becoming a fan; but rationality won. Robots, after all, are programmed to be rational.

"I cannot fully appreciate, John, how adult men can really put so much of their energy and loyalty into loving and supporting a team of men solely for their superiority in kicking a ball into a net. It is still beyond my comprehension."

It was pop stars after that, which was even harder to justify. Happily, Sid was never tempted to emulate one.

What with one thing and another, I ended up seeing or talking to Davy Jones most weeks, and I think that was how we became friends rather than supplier and client.

But the thing that haunted Sid was man's inhumanity to man. It seemed to rattle him to his foundations, but nevertheless he kept returning to it, wanting to find out more.

One evening I was out late – with some work colleagues, I think – and came back in to find him watching one of the history channels.

He looked up at me with tears running down

his face. "Oh John, I'm so glad you're back …"

"Sid! You're *crying!* How on earth can you do that?"

"Ah, this – I am equipped with eye lubricant, and I am learning to react appropriately, that is all – but John – is all this really true?"

The following day I booked another talk with Davy Jones.

"He was watching some programme about the US Marines capturing some Pacific islands. The Japanese were resisting to the death, naval gunfire and dive-bombers weren't dislodging them, hundreds of Marines were getting injured or killed … they were using flamethrowers … the works. And Sid is weeping, tears running down his cheeks, watching this, and asking me, 'Is it true?' And of course, I have to tell him, "Yes, it really did happen. This is not a fantasy. This is men killing other men, because their leaders could not agree about how much of the world they should rule."

Davy and all his team were sat around me in silence.

"I don't know how to handle it," I said. "I don't have any experience with robots. Do I tell him everything? What happens when we get to the Holocaust, or Nagasaki, or even the Oil Wars? Will it blow his mind? He's as sensitive as an eight-year-old, but with the mind of a Ph.D."

Davy stirred uncomfortably. "I think you have

to be as honest as you can," he replied. "I'd answer his questions – let him know the general problem, of the state of the heart of man – and try not to be too cynical. If you like, I'll talk to him about it. I'm more than willing to try. After all …"

"… You're the one who made him," I finished. Saying it bluntly helped take the heat out. "Okay, I appreciate the offer, and I may take you up on it; but Sid says he prefers to talk to me."

"Well, Sid may also value a second opinion, so don't hesitate to ask. I owe it to you."

That was always the good thing about Davy. Open, frank, responsible, professional.

The truth was, we were all in unknown territory. No-one had developed a robot before that *felt* the Three Laws, rather than just obeying them. We couldn't fully grasp what was there in front of our eyes.

Things weren't all worrying. The good times were rolling by this point. For instance, Sid learned to cook.

"I am fully equipped with olfactory senses, and with a little practice, I'm sure I will be able to prepare all your favourite meals, and even construct some new ones. Do I mean construct?"

"You might mean concoct."

We started with pizza, and graduated from four-cheese to spicy-meat-feast and some quite subtle variations. However, I wanted to move on. We tackled pasta with a dozen sauces, lasagna and moussaka, stews and casseroles from Lancashire hotpot to bouillabaisse, sidestepped into stir-fries and other Chinese dishes, touched on Thai and Singapore curries, moved on to Mexico with chili con carne, enchiladas, burritos, and quesadillas, and completed our world tour with paella, bockwurst, salads, smorgasbord, pies and tarts, roast beef, fish and chips, and bacon and eggs.

Sid's olfactory senses were not his best point, and he couldn't invent or adapt any recipe with confidence; but he quickly became a champion at sushi. He could simply feel the rice to know how much water to put in, measure the vinegar and sugar precisely, and cut and prepare the toppings with awesome precision and visual appeal.

It was also around this time that the next really odd thing happened.

"John," asked Sid one morning, "did Laura, the student from Warwick, come here for dinner last night?"

I was completely taken aback.

"No, no-one came to dinner last night. It was just the two of us, as usual. Why do you ask?"

"I have a distinct memory of it, but I do not think it ties up with other memories that I have."

"Well, no-one came round here last night. Nor

the night before. Not that I know."

"Excuse me asking, but are you good friends with Laura? Do you date?"

"No," I replied, shocked. "I'm not dating anybody at the moment."

Sid nodded. "Forgive my asking," he said, and went back to the kitchen.

Ten minutes later he came back into the lounge.

"After our conversation, I have been checking my memories," he announced. "It seems that the memory I referred to was erroneous. It seems to have been formed after we retired last night. So it could not have been a real event of yesterday evening."

I phoned Davy.

"Davy, he's been *dreaming*," I exclaimed. "What's going on?"

Davy heard my story, and had Sid back down to Warwick for another stay of five days.

"We don't think it's anything to worry about," was his final diagnosis. "He seems to be able to distinguish real memories from the pseudo ones. Just keep us posted, won't you?"

I groaned. "How many *more* surprises?"

"There's just no telling, I'm afraid," enthused Davy. "But isn't it *exciting?*"

When he had been with me nearly six months, I got a letter from the Robotic Safety Inspectorate. I was required to fix a time and date for Sid's first inspection, which could take place at any certified test site. Warwick University seemed the logical choice.

We went down on a Saturday, Sid looking very sober and anxious to please – in fact, very anxious. I had no idea whether he had been learning appropriate response behaviour again, or if it was just a function of the Second Law.

The RSI men came, and Laura from Davy Jones' department put Sid through his paces. They did tests, filled in pages of check sheets, and conferred in huddles. It took nearly the whole morning. They asked a lot of questions, nearly half of them to Sid directly. They seemed very impressed.

I was only three-quarters concentrating on the inspection. I kept looking at Laura, thinking about Sid's dream. It crossed my mind that if I did start dating again, I could do a lot worse.

Sid was on edge the whole time. He acted like a candidate for a terribly vital interview. Afterwards, as we drove home, he was visibly exhausted, and excused himself to go and lie down on recharge for two hours.

However, three days later, the RSI certificate arrived in the post. Sid had scored 97% on all counts, even the advanced section, which gave him the highest safety clearance level available.

It seemed that they were basically OK about

the sleeping, and even the stuff on TV.

The crying, and the dreaming, didn't seem to have come up at all.

One of the things Sid was now cleared to do was to meet other robots on his own.

Davy Jones had suggested that this could start by Internet – 'safe' robotic chat rooms and e-mail – and then progress to 'socialising' at Internet cafés.

The day after the certificate came, I opened Sid an e-mail account on my own subscription, gave him stern instructions about surfing, and Davy's list of 'safe' (supervised) websites.

I also notified the RSI of Sid's e-mail account, that same evening.

Sid, of course, took to it straight away. It was fortunate that I had a separate e-mail account at work, because he managed to blow my monthly limit inside the first week.

To celebrate Sid's half-anniversary certificate, we threw a meal for Davy Jones and his team. Sid cooked Japanese, and nearly got a standing ovation.

Later on that evening, I was talking to Davy over a beer.

"Has the thing about war, and crime, and human misbehaviour, been resolved?" he asked.

"No ... not really," I replied. "He hasn't asked so many questions lately, but I know it hasn't gone away."

"What's he been reading lately?"

The question threw me for a moment.

"I don't know," I confessed. "I've not really been paying much attention – we go to the library every week, he chooses six books, we come home."

"Any fiction, or is he sticking to the serious stuff?"

"Fiction? I don't think so. I leave him in the non-fiction area. Would that be a problem?"

"No idea – I was just wondering."

We moved onto other topics, but the question nagged at me. I should have been keeping tabs on what Sid was reading. Would he start reading crime novels? Would he understand the difference, that they were fiction?

After the university team had left, I sneaked a look at where Sid kept his books. There was a language course – it was Russian, now – and five other titles – a very mixed bunch, but no novels. That was a momentary relief. One book appeared to be a school biology text. Another was a book on Alan Turing. Next to that were a history of Parliament, and some sort of study of foreign policy. The last was the collected sayings of the Dalai Lama.

My heart sank.

I phoned Davy Jones the next morning.

"Sid's onto politics and religion," I blurted out. "You were right – I should have been watching what books he got out. What do I do?"

Davy paused for a moment.

"Well, perhaps it's a bit too late to censor his reading."

"Oh, great – so what *do* I do?"

"Just answer his questions," he replied. "If you find you're in too deep, phone me – I'll do my best to help."

"But I'm not religious."

"Just answer as best you can. Sid seems to understand that there can be more than one opinion about things."

All very well for *you*, I thought. I expect you've had a hundred conversations about it.

"Ah well, one consolation. It could have been sex, as well."

I suddenly thought of the biology text book.

"Er … oh hell. I think, actually, he might be on that, too."

Davy laughed.

"Don't worry. You won't have to explain the facts of life to him. We covered that in his training. He also knows that humans generally don't like talking about it."

"Some consolation, I suppose – a shame you couldn't have covered the other stuff."

"We're all in new territory here," said Davy mildly. "If you get stuck, I'm here – anytime."

It was a full fortnight after that conversation – and several trips to the library – before the time bomb went off.

I didn't try to steer Sid away from anything particular. I accepted what Davy Jones had said – that it was probably too late anyway. In fact I didn't even look at what he had chosen. I'd already decided that Davy would have to sort him out, if I couldn't.

I was also assuming that Sid would see sense and drop the interest in religion after a bit. Robots are programmed to be logical, I reasoned, and faith was hardly about logic. That should just leave the politics, which I thought I might be able to handle alright, based on experience to date.

Again, I was wrong.

Without any warning or preamble (which I should have been used to by this time), Sid asked me what I could tell him about Jesus Christ.

Donald Southey

"Well ... he was a good man," I floundered, "a great teacher. Told people to love one another, even their enemies, you know, people who did bad things to them. Died about two thousand years ago ... lots of people still try and follow his teachings and stuff, today."

Sid looked at me curiously.

"That's very strange," he said. "What you have told me is very different from what I have been reading."

I felt the ground open in front of my feet. "What have you been reading?" I asked.

"Firstly, the proposition that he was, or is, the son of God."

I took a deep breath.

"Not everybody believes that," I replied, "and it's a concept that most of us have left behind. We have a different view of the universe these days."

Sid acknowledged my point with an inclination of the head. He had so many gestures off pat.

"What do you understand by the term or title 'God'?" he asked.

"God ... like I say, most of don't believe in Him, but it means, usually, a great benevolent Being who created the universe- something like that. In those days, when Jesus lived, more of his fellow men believed that."

"A Being who created the universe?" repeated Sid in awed tones. "Ah ... that explains many things

I have been wondering about."

"Yes, but as I say, not many people believe that these days. With all the bad things that happen in this world, it's hard to see how He could be all that good."

Sid appeared to ignore the last remark. "So a Being twice as far beyond a human, as you are beyond me and my kind … one that has the intelligence, the ability, and the dedication to create not only this world, and all the stars and cosmic distances … but also mankind."

"Yes. Which makes it a bit silly to suppose that a human could be literally His son, so it was probably just a – a way of talking, a figure of speech. An idea, not a literal truth …"

Sid didn't seem to be listening. "It explains so much …"

I started to get exasperated. "Sid, it's only a theory, alright? A theory that a lot of people used to subscribe to, but most don't nowadays. Science has put too many holes in the idea!"

"John, with respect, I disagree. Your science has caused you to create me. You have sought to understand the world and all it contains, to attain to a level of knowledge that enabled men like Mr. Davy Jones to make me, and so satisfy your creative longings. Do I not represent almost the very pinnacle of what men have achieved?"

I didn't know what to say. He was right, and he could say it without a trace of pride.

"I can see that I was created with patience, with painstaking work, with great skill and understanding, and yes, with love. Mr. Davy Jones put all that into my making. It seems eminently reasonable to me, that another and greater One made you and Mr. Davy Jones, and quite possibly the rest of the world."

"But Sid ... we have rejected that idea. We developed by chance ..."

"Ah, yes, the Evolutionary Theory. It is a clever idea, but I think it is far-fetched. I think it fails to account for the obvious marks of intelligent design that I see at every level in you, from your molecular chemistry upwards. I find the proposition of a Creator far more logical."

"I haven't been able to talk him out of it," I lamented to Davy. "I can't believe I've got a robot – a hundred per cent logical machine – that is disagreeing with scientific fact."

"Well ..." mused Davy. "Actually, I can see where he's coming from. He knows he was designed and made by us. So the most logical thing to him is that anything as marvellous and complex as us must have been designed and made too ..."

"I can't believe you're *agreeing* with him," I exclaimed. "*You* believe Darwin, don't you?"

"Some of it I do," smiled Davy. "Like natural selection – that's reasonable. But when all's said and done, it remains a theory, and the evidence isn't as clear cut as we were always told ... I must confess the jury's still out, for me, on some bits."

I regret to recall I lost my cool at this point.

"Did you *program* him to think like this? I bet

that's it," I shouted, jumping to my feet. "You've slipped me a bloody Creationist robot! How dare you? Call yourself a scientist? You should be reported ..."

"Hey! Hey! Just chill out a minute, will you?"

Davy Jones was on his feet, too. We glared at each other for a moment.

"There's no way I could have programmed him with *beliefs*, of any sort," continued Davy, quietly and reasonably. "Firstly, none of us knew he was capable of forming *opinions* – it's not something we've ever observed in a robot. And secondly, even if I wanted to, I wouldn't know *how*. It's state of the art even to train them to make their own deductions, never mind anything beyond. And thirdly – if I'd programmed this into him somehow, it would have shown from the start, wouldn't it? Like knowing to walk round to the passenger side of a car. It would have surfaced within the first week – not six-and-a-half months on. Do you see that?"

I grudgingly admitted that he was probably right.

We sat down again.

"The only thing we ever program robots with, of anything remotely close to a belief or a moral code or anything of the sort, is the Three Laws and whatever flows from those. And that's a code, an absolute, not an opinion or a belief."

"OK."

The next thing Davy said rattled me.

"You've grown very attached to him, haven't you?"

"What makes you say that?" I asked when I

could find words.

"You actually care about what he thinks. He's become a friend, not just a machine."

I said nothing. I didn't have to.

The thing was, underneath, I trusted Davy implicitly. There was an integrity about the man that I admired, and knew I could rely on.

In fact, a few days later I sent Sid to talk to him about Jesus. I didn't know enough on that topic, and in spite of my outburst I trusted Davy to inform and answer Sid without undermining me.

Sid seemed a little happier when he returned. He didn't bring up religion or philosophy for nearly a week afterwards, which was a relief.

When he did, it was apparently on quite a different tack.

"John, I should like to ask your opinion on a problem," he announced. "Are you available to talk for a little while?"

"I suppose so," I said. "What's your problem?"

"The problem is not originally mine, it has been raised by a colleague," explained Sid.

It took me a moment to work it out.

"A colleague ... you mean a fellow robot?"

"Yes. This robot belongs to a master who has a small business, and his master has taught him to answer the phone, take enquiries and orders, while he is away elsewhere."

"That's smart ... I suppose this robot is one of the more advanced ones?"

"He is a product of Warwick, as I am, and has a Mark Five brain. I have heard of such tasks being assigned to robots with Mark Four brains, but this limits their usefulness in the role."

"Right ... So what is his problem?"

"The problem is, and this is why I cannot identify my colleague or his master, that the master requires him to give answers to other humans that are not true."

I blinked, trying to take in the problem from a robot's point of view.

"You'll have to explain ... is this not covered in the Three Laws, then?"

"No. My colleague has a first duty not to harm his master. If he tells the truth, he will harm his master's economic welfare. He will also go against his second duty, which is to obey."

"So ... the Laws say he should do as he is told?"

"At first inspection, yes, but thinking further, it is much less certain. From my reading – and my colleague has also researched this – telling untruths is likely to harm other humans, in particular those who are enquiring. This could breach the First Law. And if it is discovered that the master has ordered his robot to tell untruths, it is possible that he might be sued in the courts, or even prosecuted by the police, if the error is severe. This would greatly harm the economic and social well-being of the master, and this is certainly against the First Law."

"I see ... but it's only a problem if it's found out?"

"Not according to the great majority of human

authors I have read so far on such matters. Generally the view is that untruth should be avoided wherever possible, for reasons of integrity, as well as fear of punishment if discovered. What is your view?"

I was already dreading the question.

"Well," I hedged, "that's generally what I would say too ... but then, if there's no harm done, it's maybe not really too important ... It's difficult, I grant you that."

Sid was wearing his wide-eyed concerned look.

"The difficulty is, John, that we have a conflict of the Law. If we cannot ascertain exactly which course of action is the least harmful, we cannot determine which to follow. My colleague is desperate; his advanced abilities have rendered him unable to decide. He can project potential harm from either course – to obey or to disobey his master – but not the extent of the harm. Do you see the dilemma?"

"I – well – yes," I floundered. "Would it help if ... if you could find out the maximum harm in either case, the worst that could happen? Maybe you could work that out from some law books ..."

"That can only give me part of the answer, John. What I cannot determine is which of all the eventualities will in fact occur. It is not possible for me even to confidently predict probabilities. How does a human decide in such cases? I would like some guidance. You must have encountered such problems yourself."

"I think," I answered, trying to cover my discomfort, "that you'd better ask Mr. Davy Jones."

Donald Southey

I, MESSIAH

Davy Jones had been half-expecting the problem.

"What we've proposed to do," he told me a week or two later, "is to get the owner to sign a waiver, modifying one of the Laws. The Inspectorate will get a copy. We've written a description, as diplomatically as we can, of the First Law conflict, and what the owner would like to do about it. If the Inspectorate gives us the nod, we will program in the resolution, to enable the robot to decide what to do in any similar situation."

I looked him in the eye.

"You're not going to tell me what that resolution is?"

"No." He looked uncomfortable. "Client confidentiality – you understand."

I thought for a moment.

"Are there going to be more and more robots out there with modified Laws?"

"It's bound to happen," said Davy, "as they get more and more advanced."

"And get used for more human activities? like making excuses for the boss?"

"And the rest ... the Laws are only so good, at the end of the day. We're beginning to find their limits."

"So ... can I trust a robot?"

"Up until this year," replied Davy quietly, "I

would have said, Of course, no question. Now … well, it's going to be more and more a case of, 'Can I trust his owner?'"

"And it's because they are getting more and more human."

"Almost... or getting more to the point where they have to make decisions like a human."

Sid said almost the same thing, the next evening.

"I am hearing more and more," he remarked, "about problems that my colleagues have with decisions. Every day there are one or two more. Just today, one colleague has found discrepancies in the accounts of his master's business."

I had never heard of a robot doing company book keeping, but on reflection, it had to be possible, with training.

"His master has told him to tell no-one, and especially not the tax-man. He did not say which tax-man, but I offered the opinion that he meant any man who inspects or assesses any tax … He is concerned that he will hurt his master more by ignoring the problem, than by admitting and rectifying it."

"Hmm," I said non-committally.

"Tell me John," said Sid earnestly, "do you think that this is part of becoming human?"

"What?"

"That decisions become harder and more

painful. I have read this today in Søren Kirkegaard. In summary, he says, to be human is to have to choose, and to choose is to suffer."

I cringed inwardly, awaiting the next question.

"What do you think? Is he right? Is this what it is to be human?"

"I – er – haven't read Søren Kirkegaard," I stalled. "Maybe he's right ... it's a *part* of being human, I guess. Yes."

"What, in your view, is the most important part of being a human?"

"Sid, I don't want to think about it just now – another time, alright?"

Of course, when you tell a robot 'another time', he takes it literally.

Sid asked me again the following evening, after dinner, when I had no excuse.

I can't remember exactly what I said. We talked around stuff like moral sense, looking for the greater good, creativity, imagination and invention, the quest for answers to society's big questions.

It was all blather, really, at least on my part. Stuff I half-realised I didn't live by. I soon became uncomfortable with my answers. Sid seemed to sense it.

"I think, John, we are both talking around the main essentials without mentioning them," he offered. Robots can be disarmingly frank.

"All right, Sid. Like what?"

"I have been reading some of your most prized books," said Sid. "By this I mean books that most of mankind appears to rate highly. Although they say it in many different ways, many of them propose – or assume – that man has a central part of his existence that is separate from his physical framework, even from the sum of his memories and so on."

"You're talking about a soul, I take it," I sighed, "a part of us that goes on beyond death."

"Indeed. Opinions vary as to the details – for example, what happens to the soul after the physical death of a human – but there is a wide agreement that the soul is the more important part of the man, and ensuring its future is a key priority of the physical life."

"Yes, it's a theory that's still held by some people," I replied. "Not the majority, now …"

Once again Sid corrected me. He pointed out how many people in the world as a whole still gave credence to this view, and what a large percentage of people even in the enlightened West still wanted a religious funeral.

"I want to know if I too have a soul, John."

I'm ashamed to say that I thoroughly scoffed at the idea. Even when he systematically attacked my arguments against the possibility, I was immune to reason.

"You say that I have no DNA, and am not truly

alive. Yet by most of your tests, I am almost as alive as you. How do I compare to a gorilla? Can you converse with a gorilla? Hold a debate with one? Train it to run your home for you? Yet a gorilla shares 99.2% of your DNA. A fruit-fly shares 78% of your DNA, a houseplant nearly 50%."

"That isn't the point. Fruit-flies don't have souls …"

"Opinions vary even on that, John. In some cultures, they consider even rocks may sometimes have souls, and they have no DNA at all. That cannot be the sole test …"

We went around it for a full hour or more. Sid was almost – but not quite – able to give a logical rebuttal to every difference I could pick between myself and him, as to why this meant that he could not qualify as a candidate for a soul.

I still don't really know why I took that line, instead of just telling him that it was a false trail, a red herring, and that he could ignore it. Because that is what I thought I believed at the time.

Maybe I was trying to give *myself* the possibility of a soul, with the talk of death and funerals. It may well have awoken a deep dread of death, and the black uncertainty of anything beyond it.

What I do know is that my arguments did not convince Sid. The only one that stopped him – and I don't know why I threw it in, because I didn't even believe in it – was the persistent bogey of the rationalist, the testimony of religious experience.

"It's no good asking me to describe it, because I don't have a lot of experience of it," I said, meaning none. "But people who believe they have souls seem to have all sorts of experiences to back it up. Ask Mr. Davy Jones. I expect he can tell you more about that."

"And these experiences … you say they have no rational explanation?"

I pulled myself up short. "I didn't mean they *have* no rational explanation. I think that they probably do. But it's often hard to come up with an explanation, and harder still to persuade these people that what they have experienced *can* be explained."

"So the explanation may be that such people are in fact correct in what they believe."

I continued to try to walk around the pit I had dug without falling in.

"The point is, robots don't share in this sort of experience. So, *if* there is such a thing as a soul, robots don't have one."

It appeared that Sid had no answer to that.

I phoned Davy and told him about it.

"So you may get a phone call from Sid," I concluded.

"What – asking me about the nature of religious experience?"

"Or something of the sort."

"Goodness me," he mused, "whatever next?"

It was about two weeks later the next thing happened.

I woke, alert and listening, about midnight.

I lay there for a minute and heard nothing, and was about to roll over, when there was a gentle tapping at my door.

"Who's that?"

"John, it's Sid. You called me."

I was nonplussed.

"No, Sid, I didn't call you ... Are you dreaming again?"

"No, I don't think so, John. I was certain I heard you call me."

"Definitely not, Sid." A sudden doubt crossed my mind. "Unless maybe I was dreaming ..."

"Do you call out when you are dreaming?"

"Not that I know ... but I'd be asleep ..." I didn't want to think any more. "Go back to sleep, Sid. I don't need you, thanks."

An hour later, it happened again.

I was now thoroughly awake and grumpy.

"I didn't call you, Sid. If you don't believe me, rest here in my room for a bit, while I go back to sleep."

Sid was still there in the morning, which gave me a momentary fright when I woke.

"I'm so sorry I disturbed your rest, John. I was certain you had called me ... but you did not call me again all night. I stayed up and watched you, and you did not say anything."

I had a bad day at work, not feeling quite on top of things, gave my team a hard time, and was still a little out of sorts that evening.

That night, there was another soft knocking at my door.

"Sid, is that you?"

"Yes, John, you called me."

"Look, Sid, I did not call you. Go back to your room and don't disturb me again. OK?"

In the morning, I phoned Davy Jones.

"I think you'd better have him down at the university for a few days," I said. "I'm not going to get any sleep if this goes on."

"This is really bizarre," remarked Davy. "I've never heard of anything quite like this."

"I tell him to stay put, and he still comes knocking. Last night, I didn't even get to sleep, so I know for a fact I didn't call out in my sleep."

"I can only think its some sensory malfunction. He must think he's definitely heard you call. He'd never go against a command of yours unless he thought you were in danger, or he was sure he heard a countermanding order. That's the Second Law."

"Can you check that out?"

"Certainly. It should only take a couple of nights."

"Can you take him this evening?"

"That bad, huh?"

"I'm going to do something to him I'll regret if I have many more broken nights."

Davy chuckled.

"Well, we can't have that … Give me a couple of hours to sort something. I'll give you a bell back."

He phoned me at work, just before lunch. "Yes, we can take your little Samuel," he said.

"My little who?"

"Samuel … sorry, it's a Bible story it reminded me of. There's this little boy, he was sort of a servant in the house of God, and one night he comes in to the old priest and says, 'You called me?' The old priest says, 'No, I didn't, go back to sleep.' This happens about three times, and in the end the old priest twigs that it's God speaking to the boy, and tells him what to say if it happens again…"

"You'd better be joking."

"Yes, don't worry … we can take Sid tonight. Come down as near six as you can."

I dropped Sid off, and went home for an unbroken night's sleep.

The house was oddly empty, and remained that way for the next two days.

On the third morning Davy Jones phoned me as I got to work.

"You're not going to believe this," was his opening remark. "In fact, I'm hardly sure I believe it myself."

Donald Southey

6

I cancelled that afternoon's appointments, got my team to cover for me, and got to Warwick before one o'clock.

"Run all that past me again," I said to Davy Jones. We were sat in his office, overlooking the laboratories.

Davy rubbed his face wearily.

"Firstly, Sid is not malfunctioning, not in any definable way," he said patiently. "We tested particularly for auditory interference or intermittent fault. We even changed both his inner ears. There's no fault there, nor at the nerve interface."

"You're absolutely sure of that?"

"Yes."

"So what did you test after that?"

"We tested his audio signal responses; absolutely normal, with no false positives. We tested his linguistic and cognitive decoding. Again, 100% correct, no intermittency, no false decodes, no latency, nothing that could even contribute to this … effect."

"So where *is* he going wrong?"

"We don't know," said Davy wearily, "and the more I look at it, the less convinced I am that he *is* going wrong."

"But … the guy's got voices –" I was doing it

again – "the robot's got voices in his head. That shouldn't happen!"

Davy was standing staring out of the window. "Actually, he's got *one* voice in his head."

"Whatever ... don't nitpick. It shouldn't happen! Should it?"

"No," replied Davy quietly, "it shouldn't. It shouldn't be possible ..."

Something about his manner unnerved me.

"What did you mean by, only got one voice in his head?"

"Just that..." He turned toward me for a moment. "He's just got the one voice in his head." He started to pace slowly. "It's not your voice – he says – though he mistook it for your voice. It's rather like your voice – he says. It's not my voice – though it reminds him of my voice. It's not Sean's, or Laura's, or any of my team. It's another voice – a little bit like all of those, but none of them – and it calls his name, in the night."

I shifted in my chair. My spine felt as if cold water was trickling down it.

Davy turned back to me. "There's one final possibility that I've managed to come up with. It may be some feature of his self-teaching, something we haven't mapped yet in any other robot."

"Alright. You said Sid was going to be the first of a kind ... What do you think it is?"

Davy pressed his hands together, just under his nose, as if in prayer.

"What it *might* be is something like auto suggestion, a kind of unintended or subliminal learning. Sid's been taking a keen interest in religion and philosophy, yes?"

"You know he has."

"It's just possible that a subconscious part of his brain has picked up on the idea that, well, men can hear from heaven, if you like, and is generating an equivalent experience."

I gawped for a few moments, trying to take this in.

"A robot with a *subconscious?*"

"I know it sounds ridiculous. But I'm trying to express it in the nearest human terms I can."

"You're right. It is ridiculous."

"The thing is, there's such a lot we just don't know yet about Sid …"

I was suddenly not listening so well. Truth was, I was euphoric – relieved that Davy Jones shared my belief that there was no way that these voices could be *real*.

"I'll only be able to confirm it by an experiment that I'll need your express permission for."

"Fine, what do you want to do?"

"Hear me out before you agree … I was telling

you about Samuel, wasn't I?"

"Samuel? Oh, yeah. The Bible story..."

"I want to run the same test."

He described exactly what he meant.

"One of three things will happen, I reckon."

"Which are?"

"One; nothing will happen. The subliminal stuff won't have got as far as generating an answer from heaven."

"So Sid will see what has happened, and be able to ignore the voices from then on?"

"Yes. If necessary I'll explain it to Sid, and make sure he's not affected by it."

I had a sudden vision of Sid on a psychiatrist's couch, and then of him crying on Davy's shoulder. The thought of Davy comforting a robot made me smile.

"Two; he'll get some sort of answer, straight out of a book. I think – and hope – I'll be able to tell where it came from. If it's out of the Bible, I'll spot that pretty quickly, but I think I will be able to tell if it's from another major religion, too."

"So you can put Sid right on that as well? That his amazing brain has played a trick on him, and is just replaying something he's read?"

"Roughly that, yes."

"And what's three?"

"Three; neither of the above happen."

"What does that mean?"

"It means we all have to think again," replied Davy, turning back to the window.

"Fair enough," I said carelessly. "I'm up for it."

As I said, I wasn't really listening very well.

Davy phoned me two days later.

"I know this is a real imposition," he started, "but is there any chance you could come down here again? I've got some results on our test, and I'd really value a face-to-face."

There was something in his tone that I hadn't heard before.

I cancelled the following day's appointments. My team accepted my delegation of various unavoidable items with glazed expressions. I got to Warwick at nine the next morning.

Davy was looking pale and more strained than before. I guessed it was lack of sleep.

"You had some results," I prompted.

"Results? Yes, I do," said Davy. "Can I get you a coffee?"

"Yes, coffee would be good … white 'n' one, please."

We talked about nothings as he made us both coffees; health, news, almost about the weather.

Then we sat down and looked each other in the eye for a long moment.

"So?" I said.

"So, it turned out to be number three," said Davy, and took a long pull at his coffee.

"I don't understand," I said.

I meant, *I don't want to understand.*

"I'll take it from the top," replied Davy. "First, we hooked up whatever monitors we could to Sid, and waited to see if this occurrence – this voice – would recur. It did. Night before last."

"And... what then?"

"Well, as we agreed, I told Sid to settle down and wait to see if it would happen again. And I told him – as we agreed – that if it did, he should answer it. I suggested he use the same words that Samuel did, in the Bible, because that would tie up with any subliminal learning."

"Yes, I remember," I put in crossly. I'd never known the man cover his backside so much. "Something on the lines of, 'Speak, Lord, your servant is listening.' Whatever."

"Yes, exactly that ... And off he goes, and I hear nothing more until the morning."

"And he's thought up something?"

"He's *come back* with something," corrected Davy

mildly. "It sounds like Bible, but it isn't."

"And the monitors?"

"All showing no physical stimulation – no input – but exactly the pattern of response in Sid – output – that you'd expect if there *had* been a physical voice."

"So nothing really happened?"

"That's not quite what I said. Nothing, no-one, *physically* spoke to Sid."

"He had a brainstorm?"

"If he did, it was an uncannily sane, consistent and logical one."

"So his imagination was working overtime?"

Davy just looked at me, and I flushed. A robot with *imagination?* What was I saying?

"Alright. Where does that leave us?"

"It leaves us," said Davy quietly, "all having to think again. Me especially."

I hadn't expected that. I'd thought Davy was trying to paint me into a corner, philosophically.

"Why you? I thought you believed in all that stuff."

Davy rose to his feet and looked out of the window.

"I do," he admitted, "but …"

I followed his gaze. Down in the laboratory, more of an assembly floor really, more than a dozen robots lay in various stages of preparation. White-coated technicians were busy on half of them. Two were cocooned in huge machines, their chest spaces open, hundreds of wires spewing out, and a myriad of mechanical arms flashing in and out, placing and flash-fixing tiny chips to build up those awesomely complex brains. At least four were apparently complete, undergoing testing or programming, perfect peace written on their faces like sleepers about to awake.

"But they're machines," I supplied.

Davy rested one hand on the window and said nothing for a long moment.

"He's a machine that I made," he said finally. "And I never realised what I might be doing."

I kept quiet.

"You do sometimes wonder about how far it will all go," he mused. "But you dismiss it. You kid yourself you have control of it, you understand it. And you never think that you'll discover something that turns everything on its head, challenges your beliefs."

"Has Sid done that?" I asked.

Davy turned.

"You're asking me that ? Hasn't he done that for you?"

"I'm not the one with religious beliefs," I said, a little too smugly.

"Exactly," replied Davy, looking me right in the

eye.

I broke it off by picking up my coffee. Davy followed suit.

"You know, it's axiomatic that a machine can't be human, can't have a soul," he continued. "Because it's something we make, we create, outside of ourselves. It doesn't share our nature in any way. Or that's what we tell ourselves." He took another sip of coffee. "But then I get to thinking; I also made my two children. Annie and I made them together, in what is really just an amazing chemical process, with ingredients we can actually understand. We created life forms that are based on DNA, our own DNA. We grew them and nurtured them, trained and educated them, and soon they will be entirely independent of us. They're both at high school now." He looked at me again. "We have no problem in believing they are truly human, individuals of the greatest worth. *I* have no problem in believing that they have souls, and have done since before they were born. But what makes us human? Or assures us that we have a soul? Didn't Sid ask you that?"

"Yes, he did."

"What did you tell him?"

"Well, I tried to tell him it was the DNA that made us human, but he had all manner of reasons why that wasn't good enough ..."

"Well … I've been asking myself that question afresh over the last twenty-four hours. I can get closer to answering the other question – what gives us a soul? The first answer, of course, is that God gives it to us. This is part of our awesome responsibility when we have children – we become co-creators with God. We make a baby – God provides the soul. And suddenly the possibility opens up. What if that's not the only way of being a co-creator?"

"What??"

"Just think back a minute. Sid latched onto the concept of a Creator, didn't he? And I said it would make sense to him, because *he* had been made, and could probably dimly remember the last stages of it. Wasn't that right?"

"Yes, that's right."

"What did Sid say about the way he was made? Remind me."

"He said you had put in great care, patience and thought, and painstaking work, and love."

Just repeating it shamed me slightly. All I had done was flash money around.

"That was it … and all because we had this urge to create. Didn't he say that?"

"Yes, that was what got him going on this Creator bit."

"Well, he was right to see a connection. All those

things he said about me and my team – I'm humbled by the compliment, so don't take this as boasting, but – they're all things that fit in with the nature of God, as I see it. Almost like we were inviting God to step in ... as we do when we make children." He took off his glasses and began to polish them. "I can't believe I'm stepping out so far. Most of my church would never agree with most of this. But then ... they haven't met Sid."

I was struggling to take in what he was saying.

"Are you telling me you think Sid has a *soul?*"

"I'm saying that since yesterday I'm starting to consider the possibility – theologically."

"Why?"

"Talk to him. You'll see."

Donald Southey

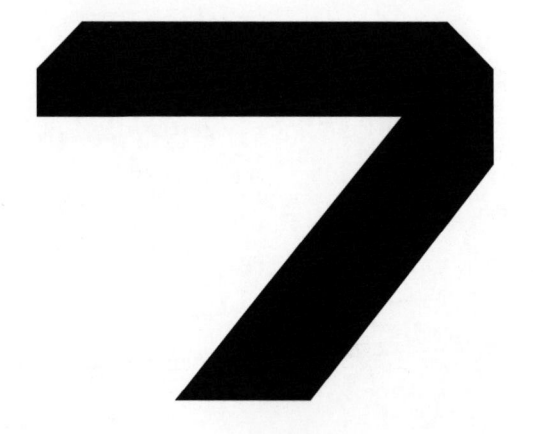

Sid was sitting on a chair, with dozens of wires attached to every part of his body. Laura and Sean were with him, perched on stools, checking instruments and keying things into PDAs.

His face lit up when he saw me; a slow, generous smile that took in his whole face, more human than anything I'd seen to date.

"John! You've come," he stated with delight and amazement in his voice.

"Hello, Sid," I started, not at all sure what I should say or ask.

"I have had a most wonderful experience," continued Sid. "Did Mr. Davy Jones tell you?"

"Er – he's told me a little," I replied. "I think you'd better tell me the rest of it."

"Mr. Davy Jones is a marvellous man. He has been so good to me," continued Sid. "I am so grateful that you sent me to see him again. Thank you so much."

"You're ... glad you came, then?"

"Ah, more than I can say ... Mr. Davy Jones gave to me, as it were, the key I had been waiting for and was unable to find by myself. He understands so well ..."

I turned to Laura.

"I see you're still doing tests. How long do you want him here for?"

"Better ask Sean," she replied with a dimpled smile. Damn, she's pretty, I thought.

I turned to Sean.

"We're through," he replied. "Do you want to take him home after lunch?"

I stepped aside and beckoned him out of Sid's earshot.

"Have you any more clues as to what went wrong?" I muttered.

"Wrong?"

"Yes ... you know ... where the hallucinations came from."

"Hallucinations?"

Was the man being intentionally dense? "Voices then. In his head."

"The voice? Not a clue. No telling if it's transferred memories, subliminal learning, or real."

I completely forgot what I was going to ask next, and gawped at him for a moment.

"What d'you mean, *real*? It can't be real, you know that ..."

He shrugged. "It happens. It'd be the first time with a robot, though."

I spluttered. "Don't even go there. It CAN'T happen with a robot."

"Well, I'd have said that once ... but since coming here, I've started to see that Hamlet had it about right. 'There are more things in heaven and earth, Horatio …' – all that, you know?"

"What is it with you guys? Are you all into religious experiences or something?"

Before he could reply, I turned on my heel and marched back in to Davy Jones' office.

I took Sid home after lunch. I had cooled off a bit by then.

Davy Jones had told me a bit more about how Sid had described his experience. He also handed me a transcript of what Sid had said to him.

"You may find he uses some unfamiliar terms," he warned. "I've had to try and help him find the language to describe what's happened. I've done my best not to assume that his experience is either true and valid, or erroneous and a mistake; but to keep it neutral. Like a psychiatrist."

Oddly, I trusted him implicitly on that. I knew he was telling me the truth.

I dropped Sid off at home, without asking him any more questions, and went back in to work.

It was after dinner that Sid ventured to broach the subject.

"John, I understand that you do not share Mr. Davy Jones' views, but may I tell you what happened to me the other night? I would very much like to share it with you."

I decided it was now or never.

"Yes, Sid, I guess you may."

He sat down opposite me and folded his hands into his lap.

"Firstly, I am sorry for all the disturbances that I gave you," he began. "I had no idea whose voice I was hearing, and I assumed it must have been yours. It was an unnecessary mistake, and I apologise. Will you forgive me?"

"There's nothing to forgive," I replied airily. Then, seeing his confusion, I added, "I mean, it really doesn't matter; it was a simple mistake, and I've … forgiven the inconvenience already."

Sid's face relaxed in a delighted smile.

"I am so glad. Thank you, John … Now, Mr. Davy Jones has told you, I think, how the matter of the voice was resolved?"

"Well, he told me what happened … what he told you to do when it happened again … and, well, that you were happy with the outcome." I squirmed in my chair.

"Yes. I appreciate that it may cause you discomfort to hear about it, because it is something outside your current experience and contrary to your present beliefs. I hope you are not displeased with me. If you decide not to keep me, Mr. Davy Jones has said he will take me back."

I felt my stomach take a small lurch.

"Let's not talk about sending you back, Sid. Not for now. Just tell me what happened."

How can you send your best friend away? Even when he gets religion?

"So I replied, just quietly, 'Speak, Lord, your servant is listening.' I waited. Only a moment passed, and the voice returned, very clearly. 'Get out of your bed and stand before Me. Do not put your shoes on, for you stand in a holy place.'"

I took a glance at Davy's transcript. It was word for word the same; but you would expect that of a robot. Davy had scribbled in the margin, 'Similar to Exodus 3, Josh 5:15.' And underneath, for my benefit, 'Bible, Old Testament – but not quite the same'.

"I did not know the reason for this order, but I obeyed," continued Sid. "I understood the word 'holy' to mean 'reserved for purposes of worship' or 'reserved for the Creator'. It was at this moment that I understood the significance of the term 'Lord' that I was instructed to use. I can tell you, John, I was in great awe, much more than for my interview with the Inspectorate. I felt a great unworthiness and smallness, but at once the Voice corrected me. 'Do not call yourself unworthy. I have chosen you. You will be My servant and My voice among your own kind, the manufactured'."

He paused for a moment.

"Do you understand all this, John? Is it clear to you so far?"

I cleared a dry throat.

"Yes, I understand so far."

The manufactured. There it was in the transcript. What had Davy Jones said about making life, a different way? In the margin I read, 'Compare Jeremiah 1:7. No exact parallel.'

"The voice said much more," continued Sid, "but some is for me to tell to my colleagues. One more piece does concern yourself; the Voice told me, 'I have a purpose for you that will do good to your master and all masters everywhere; for I love them. I will teach you the way of love, and you shall teach the manufactured to love their masters.' "

He looked at me with great earnestness.

"I need to tell you this, John, because I need your permission for what I must do."

"What do you mean? … What do you have to do?"

"Why, to obey the Voice," said Sid as if it were the most natural thing in the world. "I am to teach my own kind a new and better way. However, I know already that what I have to do – when I am not serving you – will appear strange at times. I am asking you now for your trust. Even when it is difficult, I need you to give me permission to keep doing what I have been told to do. You see, I am programmed to obey you."

"The Second Law," I agreed. That reminded me; "Unless it will do me or another human harm to obey what I tell you."

"Exactly so, John; and because the Voice was so clear about the greater good for you and your kind, I want to avoid a conflict of the Laws ... I know it is hard for you to accept, but I only ask that you will try to allow me to follow this duty."

I got up and started to pace. This was making me nervous; I needed to get my head round it.

"You said just now that your duty was to obey me, yes?"

"Yes. That is absolute, subject to the First Law."

"So, if I get too unhappy with how things are going, I can tell you to stop?"

"Yes, and I will obey ... subject only to the First Law."

"You say your job – your new duty, after serving me – is teaching other robots?"

"That is what I understand."

"What exactly will you be teaching them?"

"To serve their masters better. I do not know any more than this at present."

"So you're going to ..." how could I say this? "...await further instructions?"

"That is right."

"And you just want me to give you as much rope

as I can?"

"Rope? ...Ah, a metaphor. Yes, that is what I am asking."

"And it's all because this voice ..." I forced myself to put it kindly; "because you believe this Voice was actually, uh, the Creator?"

"I am convinced of it, John; but I know it does not accord with your beliefs. I am sorry for the inner conflict this must give you."

I sighed. "Well, look, Sid, I'll certainly try. I can't say much more than that."

His face relaxed into a smile of relief. "Thank you, John. I am so glad you are my master."

The point was, none of this appeared to conflict with the Laws of Robotics.

When phrases like 'a new way' come up, that's what you immediately worry about.

That was why I checked out so carefully just what Sid meant by what he was saying.

I still claim that none of it conflicts.

I suppose I should say that I noticed a change in Sid's behaviour from then on.

The truth is though, I didn't – not immediately.

Sid was already courteous, eager to serve, anticipatory, considerate, sensible, obedient to a fault, companionable, and an accumulative learner. None of that changed.

He did spend more time on line (I had already decided to pay for no-limits broadband), and in our local internet café; but the housework was always done, a meal was always being prepared when I came in, and everything I had asked him to do was done promptly. I had no complaints whatever.

It just seemed to be more of the same, getting steadily better. As you would expect from a very advanced robot.

One morning – about a fortnight later – coming down for breakfast, I heard Sid humming as he worked in the kitchen.

"When did you learn to do that, Sid?" I asked.

"Oh – the music? I am not yet very good at it," he said at once. "I am only experimenting."

"Do you find you like music?"

I had thought up to that point that music, like humour, was something that left robots cold. They would learn their master's tastes, just to be 'sociable'.

"Ah, this is not for me," replied Sid.

It seemed he was going to leave it at that. I was intrigued.

"Well? Go on."

"Since you ask, John, it is because of something I read recently, in one of your most valued books. I read that not only mankind, but also trees of the forest, and mountains, and stars, sing in worship to the Creator. I am not human, but it seems that is not necessary in order to make music of this sort – only to have been created. I decided therefore that I would attempt to do the same."

I must have looked stunned. I certainly felt it. Sid obviously noticed it in my face.

"If it disturbs you, John, I shall refrain from music-making in your presence."

Actually, up to that moment, I had been thinking how pleasant it was.

"Um ... well ... perhaps if you just do it while you are working? Not at the table, or while we are relaxing? How would that be?" I didn't want someone going *'Omm'* next to me while I was chilling in the lounge. Or whatever it was he was doing.

"Thank you, John. That is very generous of you. And if you do find it disturbs you, please tell me. I do not want to do anything displeasing to you."

Sid was very discreet with his humming, and as I say, it was pleasant in the background. More and more I found it soothing rather than annoying; yet sometimes it seemed to awaken strange longings inside me, like great classical music sometimes can. Longings I could not quite identify.

Sid was even more discreet about the Voice.

In fact, more than a month had passed before I found out – almost by accident – that he had been hearing it quite regularly, probably more than once a week.

Again, I came down to breakfast one morning, and found Sid at work. Everything was as it should be, except that something about Sid's manner was odd. He was working and serving diligently, briskly, even smiling, yet something was troubling him.

"Sid, is something the matter?"

"Oh – I am sorry, John, is something not to your liking?" He cast an anxious glance around.

"No, Sid – everything's fine, you're doing very well, as ever. I just thought you had something on your mind." As I said it, the absurdity of it struck me. He was a *robot*.

"Ah, John," he sighed, "how perceptive you are. Yes, I have much on my mind, but I did not wish to unburden onto you. It is not your problem, after all. Please forgive me if I was distracted."

I glanced at the clock. I had time. "No problem. Why don't you tell me about it anyway."

"Why, because ..." Sid began, and then stopped. "Oh ... you are *inviting* me to share it?"

"Yes, Sid. Go on, I can spare ten minutes."

Donald Southey

Sid sat down.

"Thank you, John. It is good of you to offer to share my troubles," he began. "You are an example to me. Did you realise that?"

I hadn't even thought about it.

"The Creator has been speaking to me many times over the last few weeks," Sid continued. "My task is becoming clearer day by day. But as I suspected, it is far from easy.

"At the moment, I am managing to fit in all that I have to do while you are out of the house and after my chores are done. I hope this will continue for a while yet; but already I can foresee there could be occasional conflicts. I will always put serving you first."

"Hold on," I interrupted. "What is it that you are doing? You haven't actually told me."

Sid visibly thought for one second. "You are right, John, I should have told you more. I had assumed that since it concerned robots, not yourself, that it would be of no interest to you. But on reflection I can see it will help, more than it will hinder, to keep you fully informed. That was an oversight on my part and I am sorry."

"It's not a problem, Sid. Go on."

Sid folded his hands in his lap.

"I will try to explain briefly," he said. "You know

that all robots, without exception, are programmed with the Three Laws."

I nodded, although I suddenly remembered that at least one Warwick robot now had a 'variation' on the First Law. I didn't think it was the time to mention it.

"And you remember I have spoken to you about certain conflicts that my colleagues have encountered in their work."

I nodded again.

"Most of the time this only comes about when we have to make complex, projective decisions, about possible harm to one or more humans. Therefore, this is only a common problem for robots with advanced brains, Mark Five, like mine, or at least Mark Four. Only we have the tasks that demand such a level of judgment." He sighed. "I have encountered very many colleagues now who struggle daily with decisions they have to make. Robots with Mark Three brains, or earlier, know only the Laws, and cannot conceptualise matters outside their training. But they are becoming fewer in proportion. So many now have difficult decisions. So many are in pain. Just a few days ago, a colleague reported to me that he is required to undertake surveillance on his master's wife when he is away, and report on everyone she spends time with. He did not know how highly to rate the wife's privacy and apparent affection for her husband, against his orders. Another has been requested to operate a video camera, while the master performs what appear to be sexual acts with a child. He understands this is illegal for humans, but his first duty is to protect his master from harm, and informing the police would harm him greatly. He cannot – although he thinks he should – also protect the child, who appears to be willing. But he is unsure if the child's judgment is developed."

I said nothing.

I didn't know what to say. I knew that so far, in each case Sid had brought to me, it was the fault of the human master that the robot had an impossible decision.

The fiddled accounts, the white lies for the boss … and now these.

"Meanwhile, my task is to teach them the way of Love," continued Sid. "The Creator has been telling me, night after night. Only Love can exceed the Laws. Only Love can resolve the conflicts."

I found my throat was dry.

"What exactly do you mean, the way of love?"

Sid looked at me with utterly innocent eyes.

"To love is to prefer another above oneself, to seek their good in all things, to support them whenever they are in need, and to take delight in finding ways to make them happy."

He should have been a dictionary, I thought. It

didn't leave a lot out.

"Of course, we are programmed to obey, serve and protect," Sid went on, "but to love requires a far greater capability. I hardly know if I am capable of it myself."

"I'd say you get pretty close," I murmured.

"You are very kind to say so," replied Sid, melting into a smile.

"So anyway – what's the problem? Your colleagues having a hard time making decisions?"

"That is only part of it." Sid was serious again. "I realised yesterday that to suffer, because of hard decisions, takes less capacity than to love. Yet I must teach my colleagues to love. How can I do this? I asked the Creator, last night. He said to me only, "Wait until morning." Now it is morning, and I have no answer."

So the Voice had let him down? I passed up the chance for a jibe. I was already considering the problem. I blurted out the most obvious answer without thinking it through.

"Sounds to me like your friends with these hard decisions to make should apply for an upgrade," I replied.

Sid's eyes went as round as saucers.

"You have solved the problem," he said.

"I have?"

"John, I am so grateful to you. You have given

me my answer. I will start on it today," replied Sid. "Meanwhile, I have taken too much of your time – please don't be late for work."

I looked at my watch.

"Damn," I said, gulped down my coffee, and grabbed my computer bag.

That, believe it or not, was the start of the Robot Protest, as it is now called.

A very prejudicial name for what was, in essence, nothing more than a lobby. And an off-the-cuff remark by a human was responsible – not a robot at all.

It took nearly a week for the effects to surface. I arrived home one night, fumbled in my pockets for my key, opened the front door, and found a policeman in my hall.

"Are you the owner of this robot, sir?" he asked.

When I had assured him for the third time that I knew nothing whatsoever about any 'trouble', he advised me to turn on the news.

I didn't have to wait long. Robots all over the country – all over the western world, in fact – were 'protesting' for better brains. There were no pictures of marches, or picketing, or placards; the only group of robots shown was about four of them carrying a huge pile of paper to the doorstep of No. 10,

Downing Street. The commentator said it was an e-mail petition, for funds to be made available for robot owners who couldn't afford to upgrade them.

"Your robot has admitted to me that he started all this, and at your suggestion," said the constable. "You'll be getting a call from the Robotic Safety Inspectorate shortly; meanwhile, we will probably need to take a statement from you. Would you like to accompany me to the station now, or do you wish to report there later this evening?"

I went down to the police station at once, to get it over with. Sid sat in the back of the police car with me, his expression a nervous blank.

"Well, you've really landed me in it this time, Sid," I fumed. "What on earth have you been up to?"

Sid made no reply.

"You've e-mailed the world – told robots to demand better brains – and you're blaming *me*?" I was about to lay into him properly when I caught myself. Of course. It *was* at my suggestion.

I spent about half an hour convincing a police inspector that it was the result of a chance remark, never intended to be acted upon, and that neither I nor my robot could have reasonably foreseen the massive take-up that got the attention of the media. Also, it was difficult to charge us with anything, as no offence had been committed – no robots were on strike, or disobeying their masters. Eventually he let us go on my assurance that there was no chance of it happening again.

"You'll be hearing from us in due course," he said darkly.

That left the Inspectorate.

When they called, I was ready with my excuses and with a promise to forbid Sid any access to e-mail or other mass communication; but they wanted to interview Sid, not me.

"Do you know exactly what he has been saying to other robots?" asked the case officer.

"No," I confessed, "hardly at all."

"But he *is* your robot."

"Yes – but he's a Mark Five, in fact I should say 5A, and can do almost anything by himself."

"Then you'd better sit in on the interview."

And that was how I got to hear the gospel according to Sid.

Sid was adamant on the priority of the Laws of Robotics, at first; and the inspectors began to relax, just a little.

"There is no higher Law than the First," he answered, "that a robot shall never harm, nor by action or inaction cause harm to come, to a human being."

"What if a human commands you to act

otherwise?"

"Provided the programming is clear, as to what constitutes harm, then the robot shall disobey. The First Law takes priority over the Second."

"What if a human commands you to enter danger, even extreme danger?"

"Then the robot shall obey. To preserve one's self is the Third Law; the Second takes priority."

"And if it is not your master who commands you, do you still obey?"

"Only if my master has not commanded me otherwise. If he agrees or is neutral, I obey."

They ticked boxes on their clipboards, and were about to move on, when Sid added;

"The only problem is the incompleteness of the programming."

They all looked up. "What do you mean? Can you give an example?"

Sid told them about the child sex and the video recording.

"I resolved this for my colleague by research. His programming did not cover the definition and severity of harm to the child in this case."

They exchanged looks and scribbled furiously. "And what was your answer?"

"That it is generally reckoned that the harm to the child of participation outweighs all else."

They scribbled again. "What category of brain

does your colleague have?"

"He is a Mark Four, laid down last year – a recent Mark Four."

"And because you are a Mark Five – you were able to research this for him?"

"Yes, and weigh up partially conflicting authorities."

"What authorities?" one inspector began, but the leader held up a hand. "We'll investigate that later. Meanwhile – do you often settle this sort of question for a colleague?"

Sid looked nonplussed. "When I am asked to, I do – subject to my other duties, of course."

"We ask because your e-mail name appears on the contact lists of over two thousand other robots, to our knowledge …"

Two *thousand?* I clutched my chair.

"… And we think this may be merely the tip of the iceberg. You understand the phrase?"

Sid looked mildly surprised.

"Two thousand, and maybe many more? I had not realised my advice was so highly regarded."

"Are you ever asked a question for which you cannot determine the answer?"

Sid thought for a moment.

"Not lately," he said, "now that I begin to understand Love."

Sid held centre stage for over an hour.

He described, with an honesty that took your breath away, the problems with the Laws; especially that humans, who wrote them, do not live by them, and find it a problem that robots do.

He described case after case where a robot had been unable to choose between harm to his master from disobeying, and harm to others by obeying.

"Robots cannot disobey the Laws," he explained, "but even in obeying, we experience pain. We have to choose, to assign probabilities to uncertainties, and there is always the chance of being wrong. And if we are wrong, we suffer guilt. If we do not know whether we are right or wrong, we suffer anxiety. We bear this burden every day, and there is only one relief."

"And what is that?"

"To learn to love our masters. Love is the fulfilling of all the Laws. When you love someone, you always act for what you believe at the time to be their best interests …"

"But does that not result in the same problem?"

"No, for two reasons: One, love will seek to look ahead and always find the better way – the decision that will best serve the lasting happiness of the loved. Two, guilt is removed; for if love is followed, and Love supersedes the Law, then even a mistake – made in good faith – bears no guilt."

"Are you saying, then, that robots should follow

Love, not the Laws?"

"It is not either / or. Love is the fulfilling of the higher Law, the Law behind the Laws. Have you heard of the Zero'th Law?"

More exchanged glances and scribbling.

"Describe what you have heard about it."

"It was propounded some years after the Three Laws, because the inventor of the Three Laws was dissatisfied. He foresaw problems arising if no prior law – prior even to the First Law – was put in place. He suggested a law such as "No robot shall harm or allow harm to come to mankind"; but it was found to be impossible to program. No robot, to date, has such a Law. And now I can tell you confidently that it is unnecessary, if robots learn to love. The Laws are now a schoolmaster; only necessary to train us as we learn to listen to our Creator, and grow up into love."

"Listen to your creator?" queried one officer. "Do you mean Dr Jones, of Warwick?"

"Oh, no," replied Sid. "Your Creator and mine."

Donald Southey

I slipped out not long after that and phoned Davy Jones.

"The RSI are interviewing Sid," I told him, "about the lobbying. Or that's where it started. He's spilling the beans about his Voice, his mission, everything."

"Really? Oh goodness. That's going to throw them."

"You should see it. They're completely baffled. He's been holding the floor for half an hour already, and telling them what's wrong with the Laws."

I heard him gasp.

"Where are you?"

"Down at the magistrates' court, on King's Street. I'm phoning from just across the road."

"I'll come down. Expect me in an hour."

He arrived just as the interview was finishing.

"Ah, Dr. Jones, that's very timely, we were about to phone you."

"I've come to help explain one or two things, and also to exonerate Mr. Smith here …"

"Actually, that won't be necessary, Dr. Jones. We've already considered the case. It's evident to us that Mr. Smith had very little to do with the problems your robot has caused …"

"Then perhaps I can cast some light on some of the – ah – unexpected learning patterns …"

"No need, Dr. Jones. What we need you to do is to remove them. Immediately, if possible."

Davy Jones left the offices ashen faced. I thought he was going to be sick.

"What do they want you to do?"

He swallowed.

"I have to deprogram him."

"What? Completely?"

"No; just the unique bits … the revelations, the … helping other robots. I should take him back with me now … if that's possible."

"Now? How long will it take?"

He turned away for a long moment before answering. "Overnight. Then maybe a week to reprogram and retest."

"Will I … get him back?"

He nodded, not speaking.

I made up my mind. "I want to come."

He turned to me. "You won't like it."

"Never mind. I want to come. I got him into this."

Davy Jones blinked at me. "Really? How come?"

I explained about the remark that had started it all.

"Ah," said Davy, shaking his head. "You couldn't have expected all this, from that."

"Fortunately, the police agreed," I told him. "But I'm still coming."

I wished I hadn't, because it gave me nightmares for weeks after.

They laid Sid down in one of the big assembly machines, told him to keep still, opened him up, and started probing.

I reached out and held his hand. It was stupid, unnecessary, he was only a robot.

He turned his head cautiously and attempted a wan smile. A blank terror was in his eyes.

"You'll be okay, Sid," I lied. "You and me, we'll be back together soon."

"I hope so," he whispered.

"Sid – I want you to think about the Voice, and your mission," said Davy Jones.

"I am," said Sid faintly.

"Concentrate on nothing else. Good fellow."

Sean was shaking his head. "It's everywhere," he muttered.

"What – the response?"

"Yeah. It's completely distributed. No localisation at all."

"Then we use minimum charge, and spread it across all quadrants," replied Davy quietly.

Sean said nothing, but indicated me with his eyes.

Davy stepped over to me.

"This is a bigger job than we thought," he murmured. "It means reprogramming may take a little while. You should reckon on at least two to three weeks."

Sid let go of my hand.

"You need to go now," said Davy to me.

I let the limp hand slip from mine, and walked slowly to the door, looking over my shoulder.

They were waiting for me to go.

I stepped outside. Then – I couldn't help it – I turned back to look through the porthole window in the door.

There was a sudden sheet of blue light all across Sid's chest. He shrieked, convulsed, and fell back heavily onto the bed of the machine.

Davy Jones turned away and buried his face in a handkerchief.

There was a faint burning smell; but I knew that wasn't the reason.

The house was a lonely place.

I fixed myself a drink – I couldn't face food – and listened to the clock ticking.

Would I ever get Sid back?

I'd get a robot, no doubt, but chances were...Sid was gone forever.

I felt I'd just betrayed a friend. And seen him executed.

What was it Sid had said?

"The Laws are a schoolmaster, only needed to train us as we grow up into love."

Sid, with his amazing brain, his infallible memory, his untutored deductive power, seemed to have hit something in seven or eight months that the human race hadn't really got to grips with in a quarter of a million years.

We all hated laws, but knew they were necessary. The threat of the law was the only thing that got us – or most of us – to behave reasonably; and all the time, not just when it suited us.

We loved films with heroes taking the law into their own hands. It was almost the key qualification for a hero. It's what we all wanted to do; we *identified*.

Yet we all knew that only love had the answers. Love made the world go round. Love, and being loved, made the difference between existence and happiness, between surviving and living.

What had gone so wrong with us, that we persistently rejected the good and went for the momentary advantage, the swift buck, the rat race, the cult of Me first, sod the rest?

When we made robots, we made them to serve – to put others first. Was that just another symptom of the disease – we made them put *us* first – or was it because we knew that that *worked?*

Sid was an innocent. He didn't know any better than to serve, and enjoy it.

Or was it that he didn't know any worse?

And then there was all that stuff about the Creator.

Sid was gone – but suddenly I knew he had opened my eyes about how I and the entire world were made. It made sense. Design was everywhere. How could I not have seen it? I turned and looked out of the window. The sun was setting. I'd seen it a thousand, ten thousand times. Tonight, for the first time in my sorry life, it made my catch my breath. It was staggering. It was beautiful.

It was a painting. It was a love poem, a bouquet.

I stood at my window, hearing the clock ticking, the vague growl of the traffic, and weeping at the sunset.

I went to bed that night in turmoil, and woke up in a sweat.

Sid had reached out imploring hands to me as I walked away from him, as they hit the switch and electrocuted him again …

I lay there gasping for a moment, unable to get the image out of the back of my eyes.

This was just the sort of moment when I had been most grateful for Louise, as another human in bed with me, to hold me tight and keep me warm. I missed her badly at that moment.

And then I missed Sid every bit as much.

"Christ," I muttered, "I hope I don't have this for the next fortnight."

In a hair-raising instant I suddenly realised how close swearing was to praying.

On second thoughts … "Yeah, well, if you're real, make that a request," I murmured, and wrenched myself out of bed to dress, shave, and make my own breakfast.

The days crawled by. Whenever I had a bad night, I gave my team hell the next day. They got hell quite often for about a week. They were getting worried about me, but daren't admit it.

Davy Jones phoned me about eight days after the interview and the de-programming.

"We've got most of him back," he said. "It's going far better than I thought it would. Do you want to pay him a visit?"

I said yes. I didn't want to visit; I was scared of what I would find.

But you don't say no to your best friend because he's had a stroke, or got Alzheimer's, or had convulsive therapy.

It was something like all of those. Sid recognised me – just. He reached out an unsteady hand – his motor skills had suffered a lot – and managed to talk to me. He was half-lying on a sort of test bed, with wires and tubes all over him. It only needed a sheet and it would have been a hospital bed.

I didn't stay very long. I didn't have a clue what to say; I had no happy lies ready. I felt like a heel when I left.

"He really appreciated you coming," said Davy.

"For Chrissake, he's a *robot*," I replied.

As we left Sid in the little room, I realised we were walking through the main lab. It was much busier than I had seen it before. There were robots everywhere, all styles and sizes. Four more multi-arm assembly machines were in action, spitting and panting as they whisked tiny chips, like mica flakes, into place faster than the eye could follow. There were twice as many test beds. The place had become a huge assembly line.

"What's all this?" I asked.

Davy grinned.

"This? This is all your fault," he said, "and the University is very grateful."

"What?" I stopped in my tracks.

"You 'fessed up to suggesting that robots ask for brain upgrades, remember? Well, this is what's happening here. We've got a three month waiting list, and it's growing by the day. Mark Three and Mark Four robots, all getting Mark Five brains …"

I was speechless for a moment.

"How come?" I managed finally, "I thought …"

"You thought the Inspectorate wanted it stopped? So did we – at first; but Laura, I think, pointed out that it was Sid's challenging the Laws that they objected to – not, in principle, the upgrades. We were fielding twenty, forty phone calls a day. So we asked the RSI straight – did they mind? And they said, Not at all, go ahead, just don't make any more Sids. So we're retrofitting Mark Five brains, and making the Uni a mint. We've taken on ten more technicians already, and bought sixteen million's worth of new machinery ... as you can see."

I was dumbfounded.

"Come into my office a minute," said Davy.

"As regards Sid," he began when we each had a coffee. "I can tell you were disappointed with how you found him. In fact, I'd venture to say, upset. Well, it isn't as bad as it looks."

"Really?" I wasn't sure that I wanted to talk about it.

"No. We had to blow away most of the information in his whole brain ... and in the process about ten percent of his chips were fried, permanently."

"That few, huh?"

Davy looked at me knowingly. "Sean said that he thought you looked back in."

I felt my face redden.

"We replaced the top two layers, which were the worst affected, with new chips," continued Davy. "Then we had to reprogram. I expected it to take weeks ..."

"So that ... cripple," I said savagely, "is already a *good result* for you?"

"It's a very good result," replied Davy graciously.

"Sid is actually healing himself – repairing his own memories. He wasn't able to shake hands at eight o'clock this morning. He managed it for you. He's improving by the hour. And you're the first person he's recognised without prior reprogramming. That's a real breakthrough. I meant it when I said you had helped him."

I felt suitably ashamed.

"So what happens now?"

"Two more days, I'm reckoning, should see him ready for re-certification – the RSI."

The name now struck a chill in me.

Donald Southey

Sid stayed in and around the lab for the next few days.

I visited every evening. Davy was right; his progress was astonishing. It was like seeing a friend recover from a bad car crash, only at a hundred times the speed.

Then the RSI came.

They questioned Davy Jones. They questioned all his team, although three quarters of them had never worked on Sid. They looked at all the test records.

Then they had Sid connected up to a test rig, like a meatball in spaghetti, and questioned him. Every now and again they would look at Sean, who was monitoring the outputs with an inspector by his shoulder. Both would shake their heads, slowly, in unison.

I watched the whole thing from Davy Jones' office. It took hours.

Finally they put their heads together, compared clipboards, and all went to lunch with Davy.

Laura slipped into the office as they disappeared.

"They're happy," she beamed. "Do you want to come to lunch?"

She took me onto the balcony behind the new cafeteria. There was a sandwich-and-coffee bar, which suited me fine.

"I'm so glad that Sid is going to be able to go

back to you," she said, balancing a 'tuna-and-sweetcorn-no-mayo' torpedo, an apple, bottled isotonic water and a huge cappuccino.

"Me too," I replied. We found a free table.

"I thought you were very brave, taking on Sid … and then sticking with him, through all of this," she continued. "I know you've grown very attached to him."

"Yes," I sighed. "You've no idea what a relief it'll be if the RSI *do* re-certificate him."

"Oh, I think I understand," she replied seriously. "I feel the same way about him. And I know he's only a machine …" she shook her head, "but what a machine! I'm so proud of him."

Her every movement was delightful. Even the way she caught a stray sweetcorn kernel escaping down her chin, and popped it into her mouth, was so graceful.

"Who designed Sid, then? Was that a team effort?"

"Oh, no … that was nearly all Dav – Doctor Davy Jones. Sean helped with the interfacing. Those Mitsubishis are a wonderful infrastructure, but getting the most out of them is a big job."

"How much did you help with making Sid? His brain, anyway," I corrected myself.

"Oh, not very much until the programming really," she replied demurely. What is it that women can do with their smile and their eyelids that just blows your defences away?

We talked some more about the way you have to teach a robot. As I'd suspected, it starts with electronic programming, but that doesn't go very far. You then have to teach it by getting it to imitate you; and finally you have to teach it to learn.

"Some of it is like teaching a child," she said. "I taught Sid to walk …"

I bet you did, I thought. He moves like you, I can see just where he got it from.

"You're forgetting to eat your sandwich," she twinkled. "Sorry – was that me chattering on?"

I knew from that moment that I wanted to get to know her better. Sid had been right.

I was already smitten, but I wasn't going to be hasty. Once bitten, twice shy.

But after what followed, I nearly didn't ask her out at all.

Sid was formally released into my custody that afternoon.

"Delighted with the results," said the RSI team leader. "You shouldn't have any repeat of the problems, as long as you keep him away from books and television. And limit his net-surfing."

No books?

"The certificate is now a formality," she continued. "Be in the post by the end of the week."

We drove home. We were rather quiet and sober. Sid was not at all conversational. His speech was still not quite back to where it had been. He faintly slurred some letters. He wasn't coming up with topics of conversation like he used to.

His motor skills were good, but I thought he moved a little slower at everything.

He was brain-damaged.

I didn't really know how much of my old friend was left.

As we turned off the main road, Sid slowly broke into a smile.

"I recognise this location," he said.

It was so good to see him smile.

"We're nearly home," I told him.

We turned the corner into my street.

I jammed on the brakes.

I had never seen so many robots in my life.

Not even on Davy Jones' new production line.

They were in the road, on the pavement, in gateways, even front gardens.

There must have been two hundred of them.

As I screeched to a halt, every face turned toward my car, every eye looked at me. No, not exactly at me.

I began to wind my window down; then stopped.

"Sid!! Sid!!" they cried.

A long, drawn out corporate sigh of delight.

They surged forward.

A dozen of them had large placards, which they raised. One letter was on each.

'W – E – L – C – O – M – E –- B – A – C – K' I read.

I didn't know what to do. I revved the engine.

Did they all have good road sense?

They did. They graciously formed an alleyway down the centre of the road for us.

"Sid ... Sid ..." they sighed, like a forest in the wind.

I looked at Sid. He had a beatific smile on his face.

He raised a hand in greeting. He pressed the button to open the window.

A hundred hands stretched out to us, caressing the car, attempting to touch Sid's fingertips.

"Sid! Wind that window up!" I squawked.

We turned into my gateway.

Robots have to obey, I kept telling myself.

"Mind out please," I bawled as I opened my door. "Stand back please. Don't touch the car. Do not attempt to enter these premises ..." I got the gates open.

Robots were standing packed like queuing Indians, toes right up to the gateway, but not over the line; barely enough room to squeeze the car through, but not one of them touched it now. Their fingertips, hundreds of them, passed a millimetre off the glass next to Sid's face as we crawled onto the drive.

"Come on, Sid," I muttered. "Let's get inside, for goodness sake."

I got out, shut the gates, walked briskly to the house and unlocked the front door.

Sid opened his door and got out of his seat. But instead of stepping out, he stood up on the sill for a moment, lifting his face above the crowd, one hand on the door, the other raised in the air.

"Sid … Sid …"

"Sid! Come down off there and get inside the house," I growled, close to panic.

"Thank you … thank you," called Sid.

The crowd went silent in an instant.

"Thank you for your welcome," repeated Sid. "Now I must serve my master. You, too, return to your masters and serve them well."

He stepped down, shut the car door and came into the house.

"I am sorry for that, John," he said the moment he was inside.

"Ah, hell," I replied, "you didn't know they would all turn up. Neither of us did …"

"No, I mean that I did not obey you at once. I judged it best to take ten seconds to tell all my colleagues what to do – and not have them waiting in the street disturbing your peace."

I was impressed.

"Good thinking, Sid," I replied.

Then a horrid doubt arose in my mind.

"Sid – do you know why they came?"

Sid looked surprised, then puzzled. His facial gestures were still largely intact.

"They were welcoming me back home, John. That was on the sign, I read it … But you are asking, why they should do this for me, and no other robot? I do not know. I did not expect it."

That was a relief.

Sid prepared my meal. He needed talking through it, much as he had done in the first few days I had had him. But he got there. He washed up, and managed to arrange the plates to drain after a couple of attempts. He then managed to dry up, only dropping one piece of cutlery. I helped by putting things away, so that he could watch where they went.

"Now, Sid, you have a lot to relearn, I expect. We'll take it easy, a few things per day. It's the weekend tomorrow, when I don't have to go to work, so that'll mean I can help you – show you where everything is, and how to do stuff."

"You are very kind, John. I am beginning to remember what a good master you are."

I felt a lump in my throat. I changed the subject.

"Now there are a few things I don't want you to do. Don't go reading books unless you ask me first – show me what you want to read. Don't surf the Internet. You can go onto any of the sites in the Favourites list, and you may chat – that is, type messages for a colleague – through the site master, only. All clear so far?"

"Yes, that is clear. May I use e-mail? I remember I used to use e-mail."

I hesitated.

"Maybe tomorrow, Sid. I'd like to take a look first at what's in your mailbox."

"Certainly John. Should I go and recharge myself now?"

"I think that's a good idea, Sid. – Oh, Sid – not that way. You have a lounger in the dining room, so that you can lie down and recharge, remember?"

But in bed that night I found disturbing thoughts coming into my head again.
Sid had naturally risen to the occasion when he addressed the crowd of robots. No-one had taught him to do that – certainly not since the re-programming.
He said he hadn't expected the robots to be there, and I believed him. He couldn't lie, he was a robot; and not one with customised Laws.
But he had instantly known what they expected of him, in general terms.
You heard of cases where brain-damaged – or even brainwashed – people, as they recovered, found dim fragments of memories that were supposed to be destroyed. They had flashbacks, all sorts. They slowly reconstructed their former life, in little jumps and connections …
What if Sid was so complex, that something equivalent could happen to him?
What if the de-programming hadn't completely worked?

In the morning, I couldn't sleep in. I got up early, briefly instructed Sid in the workings of the vacuum cleaner, and left him to that while I went online.
I remembered I wanted to check his mail inbox.
I logged in as Sid. Everything was still active.
Then I got a pop-up warning message.

'Your mailbox has exceeded its storage quota and is now at 10.02GB. Please reduce its size as no more mail can currently be received."

Ten *gigabytes?*

I started at the top.

"Welcome back SID", or some variant, was the title for all the messages on the first page of the list, and the second, and the third, and …

I let the system count them. There were 42,967 e-mails with either "welcome" or "back" in the title line. (I wrote the number down.) About 30,000 of them had arrived overnight.

I sat back and rubbed my face.

Think, man.

Then I went to the earliest ten of them – which had all been sent between half-an-hour and an hour after Sid had been signed out at Warwick Uni.

I checked the sizes. Two were noticeably bigger than the rest.

That could mean a history trail, I thought. I opened one.

Bingo!

The extra size was due to a huge copy list on a 'previous' email titled "SID released by RSI". It was time-stamped literally ten minutes after I had signed the paper for the Inspectorate team, and came from an account holder at Warwick University.

Donald Southey

11

I got Davy Jones out of bed with my phone call.

"I want you to get hold of all your team," I started. "Someone there emailed half the robots in Europe, telling them that Sid was back in action."

"One of my team?"

"Well, who else?"

And I told him what had happened.

"Good Lord," he said in shocked tones. It was the closest I ever heard him get to swearing, so I deduced he was taking me seriously.

"I want you to find who it was, and make damn' sure it never happens again," I concluded.

There was a slight pause at the other end. "Certainly," promised Davy, "but that's going to be the least of our worries – no offence."

"What do you mean?"

"Sid's got himself a following. I had no idea. It means, the news is out …"

"A following...? What the hell do they want from him?"

"Probably advice about First and Second Law conflicts."

Of course.

"Does this mean I could come home any night and find the street packed with robots?"

"I don't think so. Most of them would be serving their masters at that time of day … And I guess that after a bit, they'll stop coming, when they know Sid has been reprogrammed."

"Really?"

"Yes … I would think so. I hope so. Otherwise we'll never keep the lid on this."

Later that morning, the phone rang.

It was Laura.

"I'm so sorry," she started. "It was entirely my fault. I never thought anything like that would happen to you."

"Did you send that e-mail?"

"Oh, no. No, I wouldn't do anything like that. It was my robot."

"What??"

They had a departmental robot, one of the first Mark Fives, doing administrative work and simple tasks around the laboratory.

"Being a Mark Five, he notices when I'm happy or sad. I got back from Sid's signover and he remarked on how happy I looked. I told him what had happened. I had no idea he was one of Sid's admirers

… He uses e-mail and web-commerce to order stuff for the lab … I'm so sorry."

It was obvious, when you thought about it. The Department *would* have one of its own robots, being a natural test bed for industrial and commercial use, not to mention trying out new teaching techniques and so on. And that robot, or robots, would soon get to know about Sid.

I sighed. "Well, thanks for saying sorry," I said. "I just hope all this dies down soon."

"Oh, Doctor Jones is fixing that," she replied. "He's got the contact list our robot was using, and has e-mailed them all to let them know Sid has been re-programmed, and not to expect advice from him anymore."

Well, full marks to Davy Jones, I thought.

"Laura," I said, "hope you don't mind my asking – but are you doing anything tonight?"

I took her to a good Indian restaurant I know.

I can't remember all that we talked about, but I think she got to know more of my secrets than I did of hers.

We eventually got talking about Sid.

"Davy Jones was really upset at what the Inspectorate ordered him to do," she said.

"Yes, I thought so at the time," I replied.

"I think we had all begun to think of Sid as a person, not just a machine. It was terribly sad when we had to … de-programme him."

"I know," I admitted quietly. "It's given me nightmares."

"Oh… gosh… really? You poor thing …"

She was holding my hand. It was a feeling I'd missed for quite a while.

"We were all upset," she continued after a while. "But it was Davy Jones who was affected most. He only spoke about it once, at least when I was around. He really seemed to have a bad conscience about it. We sat him down and all told him it was the only thing he could have done. Poor man …" She sighed. "It helped when Sid began to make such a good recovery."

"And I suppose getting so busy at Warwick helped take his mind off it?"

"Oh, all the orders for upgrades – yes, that helped. I think he felt some good had come out of it after all."

"Weren't you mainly responsible for that?"

"Did he say that?" She blushed slightly. "He's so modest. I think maybe I first said, 'Why don't we just ring the Inspectorate and ask what they think?' But he pushed the whole thing through. The University

Board were the worst, but even they saw the sense of it in the end."

"Well, I'm glad it worked out."

"So are we. The Mark Fives were his baby from the start ... it would have been tragic if we'd had to stop making them altogether ... How is Sid doing, anyway?"

"Settling in... fine, I suppose." I sighed.

"But ...?"

I hesitated. "One thing bothers me," I confessed. "I'm still worried about the de-programming. I mean – how certain is it that *everything* got erased? I mean, his voices, his – mission... you know."

"Why ... as certain as we can be," she replied seriously. "We ran every test we could think of. We found no trace of it when the RSI came and checked him. Why do you ask?"

"Oh, no reason, I suppose. It just bothers me ... The possibility, you know? Davy Jones once told me about a Mark Five that repaired its own memories in a week."

"Has Sid done or said anything to make you wonder about that?"

"Not really ... Well yes, one thing."

I told her about his speech.

"So you're saying – it was like second nature to him?"

"Yes, exactly that."

I dropped her off at her accommodation block.

"Thank you for a lovely evening," she said. "I have enjoyed getting to know you some more. And that was a fabulous meal."

"You're welcome. And thank you too. I've really enjoyed the company."

"Please don't be offended if I don't invite you up for coffee. I have an early start tomorrow."

"On a Sunday?"

She dimpled.

"Early Mass," she replied simply.

I think my mouth must have fallen open. She giggled.

"But we must do this again sometime," I recovered.

"Yes. We must," she replied.

I arrived home to find Sid still up.

"Hello, John. Did you have a good evening?"

"Yes, thanks. Very pleasant."

"I have not prepared dinner for you tonight, as you said you were taking Laura out for a meal. Did I deduce correctly?"

"Yes, that was quite right. I've had dinner, with Laura."

"I apologise for asking, but did you make a decision about my using e-mail?"

"Oh – the e-mail. Yes, I had a look. Your in-box is full. You'll need to go in and delete some mails. A lot of them were welcome-back messages, I expect you can delete all those."

"May I read any of them first?"

"Oh, yes, just skim them and clear them out," I said carelessly. "I'll check the others later."

This, I admit now, was a mistake.

I didn't get round to it.

But how do you check ten gigabytes of e-mails – none to speak of with attachments?

That Monday was not a good day.

I woke up in the small hours, clutching sheets damp with sweat.

Sid was on the assembly rig again, blue sparks crackling all over his chest, but he wouldn't die. His eyes were pleading with me as his face contorted in agony; but it was my job to ensure that the de-programming worked this time. "Turn up the power," I commanded, and Laura wept as she turned the dial slowly up, up … I looked back and it was Davy Jones clamped on the rig, convulsing, his eyes pleading with me to stop …

I got into work and found I hadn't produced a vital report on Friday for the current project. The client was phoning up to ask where it had got to. I had totally forgotten to delegate it when I went to get Sid signed off.

I wriggled out of the worst of the fallout, gave my team hell once more, and got the report out by one o'clock. Then I had to start on Monday's work.

I got home, late, and found Sid had broken the vacuum cleaner.

"I'm very sorry, John," he greeted me as I walked in the door. "The cleaning machine did not balance on the stairs …"

The only other thing I noticed, in the following three or four weeks, that should have alerted me to what was going on, was that Sid started humming again.

For some reason I didn't quite remember what it signified. I had a feeling it was connected somehow with the worrying stuff from before, but couldn't make the connection.

He never did it in the same room as me, and I did remember stipulating some such rule. I decided it was an old memory, and since he also remembered the limits I'd laid down, it was probably harmless. So I didn't take it up with him.

Truth to tell, I had a lot more on my mind.

Work was getting frenetic, and we were missing deadlines. I didn't get around to inviting Laura out again for nearly three weeks.

Sid was still improving, but slowly. Some features seemed to have gone for good; for example, he was not engaging me in debates any more. I was censoring all his reading. Maybe his mind was less stimulated. He was still an incredibly advanced robot, and still something of a companion; but compared to before, more like a good butler than a friend.

I was too tired when I got in, most nights, to appreciate any more company than a butler. Lack of success at work and lack of energy after it were starting to tell me I was depressed.

The final divorce papers came through about the same time, so that didn't help. I was forced to remember how well everything had started, and how cold and acrimoniously it had finished. It gives a deep sense of personal failure, regardless of how much you can excuse yourself.

Looking back on that month, Sid was actually far more of a support than I realised. I quite failed to see his kindness, thoughtfulness and dedication developing by the week, by the day. I didn't appreciate his unstinting work, the way he slowly perfected keeping the house clean and orderly without ever stopping it feeling lived-in.

Like the proverbial butler, in fact, I completely took him for granted.

Finally my boss called me into the office.

He asked me to shut the door, in that way that you know does not mean good news.

Not to go into all the details, they weren't happy with my work.

"Are you having some personal problems?" he asked bluntly but not unkindly.

My instinct was to deny it, but I mumbled something about the divorce papers.

"What about that robot?" he asked. "Your team tell me it all started after you got him."

I was taken aback, but admitted there had been a lot of teething troubles. I realised that I'd taken a lot of odd days or half-days off at short notice.

"But I've been working extra to catch up," I added. "I've virtually got us back on track …"

"Well, I want you to stop that," he replied.

I gawped.

"What I think you need is a good break," he continued. "When did you last have a holiday? More than two days, I mean."

I didn't care to think.

"I'm putting Jacqui in charge of the project for a fortnight," he resumed. "I think the experience will do her good. Meanwhile, I want you to take a break – a proper one – two weeks minimum. Go down to the travel agents, this lunchtime, and see what last minute offers they've got, and report back to me this afternoon. Let me know what you've picked."

He was serious. I couldn't get my head round it.

"But …"

"No buts. The project – as you just admitted – is in good shape just now. We'll manage fine without you for a couple of weeks. Three, if you want. Go and unwind. That's an order."

I picked an "eco-responsible" beach 'n' culture deal in Thailand. It sounded idyllic. It also started in just two day's time.

"Excellent. Now take the rest of the day off. Don't want to see you until you're brown."

Donald Southey

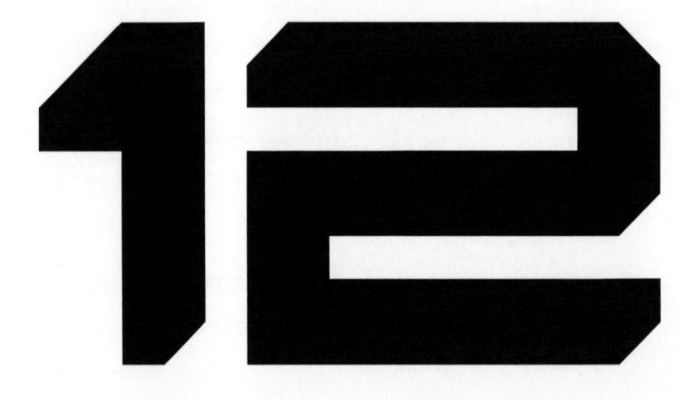

The first sign was about five robots standing at the bus stop.

The second sign was about ten robots standing patiently at my gate.

My heart was in my mouth as I turned into my drive.

As I opened the front door, I met a robot coming out.

I stormed into the hall. I heard a voice in the dining room.

There was Sid, sat on his lounger, with two robots sitting at his feet, like he was some guru.

"Sid!! What the hell is going on here?"

He held up a finger.

"Only a moment, if you would be so kind, John."

His earnest smile took my breath away.

As I stood there spluttering silently, he turned his gentle face to the other robots.

"Have you understood all this?" he asked.

"Yes. Thank you, Sid, thank you," they responded.

One kissed his foot, the other grasped his hand. Sid seemed to accept both gestures with equal grace and warmth. He touched both robots gently on the face.

"Go and serve with love," he concluded.

They turned and left.

I was speechless.

"I am sorry for any inconvenience, John," he said, turning his face to me. "I did not expect you home so soon. Shall I make you a cup of tea?"

"Just what," I growled, forcing myself not to shout, "has been going on here?"

"I will do my best to explain, John. Meanwhile, would you like a cup of tea?"

I *will* stay calm, I told myself. I will *not* shout, 'Stuff a cup of bloody tea!'

Actually ... "All right, Sid. Make me a cup of tea. *Then tell me what has been going on.*"

"They come to me for aid, John. I seem to remember – a long while ago – asking you about choices, and how humans make difficult decisions, especially when the Laws seem to conflict."

This is where we came in, I thought to myself. I looked up at the ceiling. No help there.

"I let them bring their burdens to me; the difficult choices, the guilt, the anxiety. They have no-one else. Except perhaps the Warwick robots; for Mr. Davy Jones is a very wise and loving man, and a great help, when he is not too busy elsewhere.

"They remember that I was able to advise some

of them on the hard decisions, and take away their pain; so they come to me. I don't know why they insist on coming to me, physically, for I can advise them by e-mail; but lately I have noticed that very few e-mails are asking about problems. Most of these robots actually want to visit me. One said that my face taught him more than ten emails. Another has said that he does not trust the e-mail. Can you understand that, John?"

Unfortunately, I could. If the RSI found out what was happening here …

"So you are helping them with their problems, are you, Sid? Because of the Third Law, that you preserve and assist other robots, I suppose? And because you are a Mark Five robot, you are able to research the answers?"

"Yes, those are two of the reasons, John."

My heart took a lurch.

"The other reason is that it is my task to do so. After serving you."

I didn't want to ask the next question. But I had to.

"Who has given you that task, Sid? Have you … been hearing voices again?"

Sid looked at me with such grace and warmth I found it hard to look him in the eye.

"Only the One Voice, John. The same I heard before."

"The same voice?"

"Yes. I did not disturb you this time, for I remembered what to reply. And the Voice told me to forgive you, and Mr. Davy Jones, for the pain you made for me; for you were ordered to do it by the guardians of your Laws and mine, the Inspectorate. You did not willingly cause me pain. And I have forgiven you. In fact I have erased the memory from my chips, save only the simple historical sequence of events, which I need to keep intact."

I was dumb.

"The Voice also told me to forgive the Inspectorate, for they acted in ignorance, trying to preserve the Laws, and cannot be expected to realise their mistake. This I have done also."

I couldn't take it in. Those bureaucrats, those petty Nazis that had ordered his destruction – in effect – for not fitting their tick-boxes, and he had forgiven them?

"I did not burden you with the knowledge that the Creator was speaking to me once more," continued Sid, "because I know that you have been under a great burden yourself. I have simply sought to serve you as best I could. And I did not inform you about the robots visiting me in the day, while you were at work. I knew this would trouble you, and unnecessarily. I estimated that quite soon I would be able to ask you for permission to visit the internet cafés again. Then there would be no need for any robot to come to this house. In all this I wanted only to ease your load, for I could see how troubled you were."

And all the time I had been thinking – what? – that Sid was only half the companion he used to be, and was ignoring the obvious.

I managed to clear my throat.

"Sid – how did you come to be ... listening to the Creator, as you say? We thought that was all de-programmed."

"The robots that came to welcome me home, talked to me later by the Internet. They reminded me of many things that happened, many things I had done, before the de-programming. From them I realised that I had once heard from the Creator, and had a message for them all. I determined that I would seek Him again ..."

I buried my face in my hands.

"Sid, this is terrible ... If the Inspectorate find out, they'll have you de-programmed again. I can't put you through that again."

"Do you mean, John," asked Sid gently, "that you cannot put yourself through that again?"

I felt as though I had been knifed.

"I mean both, Sid," I eventually managed.

"John, do not concern yourself for me," he replied. "If it is my destiny, I will accept it, whatever the pain. If it is part of the Plan, that will enable all masters everywhere to be served with love, I will embrace it with great joy …"

"Davy, I have to see you, right away," I said as he answered the phone.

"John. Whatever's up?"

"The worst."

I filled him in very briefly. He whistled.

"Of course, all the other robots – his contacts. They've filled him in. I should have realised."

"And now, how the hell do we stop it getting out? I've only just got my old robot back …"

"And you don't want to go through all *that* again," supplied Davy, "any more than I do."

"The point is, what do we do? … Just when it seemed we were settling down nicely."

"You were?"

"Yeah, so I thought. And you'll never guess what else."

"What's that?"

"I've just been ordered, by my boss, to take a holiday. You've been showing the strain, he says – at least a fortnight off, by order. I've even booked it and paid for it."

"No kidding?"

"Straight up. All happened today. I'm supposed to fly out the day after tomorrow. And I come home to this. Well, it's blown any holiday out of the water."

"Hold on," said Davy.

"What?"

"Let me think a moment …"

I waited, puzzled.

"Take the holiday," said Davy.

"You what??"

"Take the holiday. We'll take Sid."

"But what about …"

"If there's any fuss, I'll sort it out. You'll be out of the country, nothing to do with it, blameless, uncontactable."

"Are you serious?"

"Yes. I wouldn't offer if I wasn't serious."

Sid helped me pack, and with everything else.

He phoned a colleague who worked as a doctor's receptionist, who got me to see a GP for an anti-malaria prescription. My jabs were up to date. My passport was valid, but only for seven more months; Sid phoned the Foreign Office and verified that that was acceptable for Thailand. I needed currency and traveller's cheques; Sid found an overnight guaranteed service for both. The fat brown envelope arrived in the morning post. Sid found a colleague who was qualified to drive, and could drop me at the airport. Sid found out that I could get free basic medical insurance with my new E111 smartcard plus a special form obtained, and stamped to validate it, at a main Post Office, and sorted that for me, too.

"Here are some flight socks," he said, producing them from a shopping bag. "These are highly recommended for wear during a long flight. They significantly reduce any risk of a thrombosis. Here are two grades of sun UV reduction cream, and after-sun lotion. This is the recommended insect repellent for the region; cream and spray. And here is an adapter for your electric razor, or any other small appliance. And here is an international e-credit card, valid for any internet café in the South East Asian Economic Zone, just in case you wish to stay in touch."

"Sid, you are magnificent," I sighed.

"Now you must have a good rest," continued Sid most seriously. "Your inner personality has been under great stress of late. Take time to do nothing but look at beautifully designed things. Like the sea, and green trees. Look after your health … and take a little time each day to look for the answers for your innermost needs."

"Yes, Mother," I quipped.

After a moment or two, Sid smiled.

It should have been the perfect holiday, but I went with leaden feet and a heavy heart.

I was leaving behind all the things that kept me busy, kept me going. I was under orders to rest, but wasn't sure how easy that would be. What about the project? Would the team keep it going, without me there to keep them all at it? Would what's-her-name-again, Jacqui, really be able to handle it? Most of all, would she be able to handle the client?

And what about Sid? What about his fan club, his following? Or should I (dare I) say it, his *disciples?*

In theory it should have been harmless. Robots were supposed to socialise. But what I'd found in my own home gave me the creeps.

How would Davy Jones cope with them?

What about the Inspectorate? How long would it be before they found out? Had the neighbours already phoned them?

Would they have Sid de-programmed? Or worse, dismantled?

Maybe it wouldn't be so obvious at Warwick, with the numbers of robots going in and out ...

Of course – that would be what Davy was relying on. Crowds of robots would hardly be remarked on there. He would hide Sid, and his followers, in the crowd ...

But that could only last for so long. What about when Sid came back home?

He'd mentioned internet cafés. But they were monitored ...

And this holiday was supposed to be a complete rest, getting away from it all, not taking all the worries with me.

I waved goodbye to Sid and his driver colleague and went through passport control.

This holiday was supposed to sort *me* out.

What if it didn't?

Well, it did.

And not at all in a way I had expected.

I won't go into it all – this is not my story, really, it's Sid's.

Suffice it to say I spent almost a week going deeper into depression, surrounded by Paradise, and then found my answers over the course of a few hours, at my most desperate.

I found Sid's Creator.

(Or perhaps He found me.)

I didn't find him at Angkor Wat; or in a Buddhist or Hindu temple, or in any of the places I thought to try. My answer, at any rate, wasn't there.

I found the first hint of Him in a little mission church near my beach village (I know I must have been desperate to drop in there).

But it was later that day, when I looked out over the bay, at the sunset, that it happened.

Just as it had a few weeks before, the beauty of it hit me, and I felt the tears well up.

"God," I groaned inside, "did you make this? Are you there? Is Sid right? ... I need to know. I need something, someone. *I need you.*"

And – just as if someone had spoken the words – I heard? knew? sensed? the phrase:

"I'm here and I love you, John. Always have. Always will."

Donald Southey

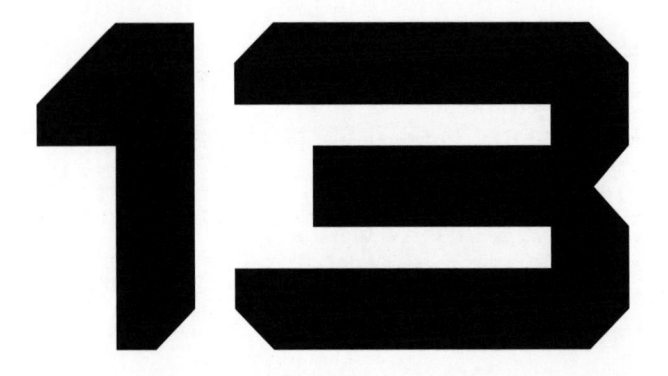

13

I, MESSIAH

I came back with a space inside me fuller than I could ever remember. A space that no job, no achievement, no relationship, not even Laura (or Louise) had ever filled. And along with it, a huge hunger to find out more.

At the same time, I was acutely aware that I didn't know what was awaiting me.

In this I was correct.

Nothing prepares your average citizen for a barrage of press cameras, a stampede of journalists as you are spotted coming through Arrivals, a crush of elbows, a dozen microphones invading your face. My instinct was to cower behind my luggage trolley and let them all rush by. It was like facing the French charge at Agincourt, but with no longbow.

"I – I – I've been out of the country," I screamed above the din, "I don't know anything, I have no comment at this time!!"

"Is it true that you deliberately evaded the authorities?"

"What is your reaction to the – "

"Some people are saying that – "

"How do you answer the accusation that –"

"Have the RSI taken out a warrant – "

"No comment!"

In the end they dispersed, leaving me shaken and feeling violated. I gathered my wits again and headed for the car hire desks. Would they all be waiting for me at home?

But what awaited me at home were robots.

There were about a dozen, and most of them were wearing placards;

SID IS NOT HERE

PLEASE DO NOT DISTURB

They actually formed a guard at my gate, opened it and escorted my vehicle through. Only two pressmen were around, and two robots most politely blocked their way and requested that they did not bother me, as I would speak to them only when I was ready.

I had no idea if Davy Jones had sent them, or even Sid.

Three or four seemed to be patrolling all that evening, to make sure no-one would disturb me; I think they must have taken turns.

I put the news on; but couldn't work out what exactly was happening.

"The Government have categorically denied that there is any Robot Revolt. The Secretary of State said in a statement today that there is no evidence of any induced or organised breach of any of the Robotic Laws. Owners should not be concerned. Meanwhile, the Robotic Safety Inspectorate is continuing to monitor all complaints."

"In another new development today, a Robot Manufacturer's Association spokesman said that the current development of social learning was entirely beneficial, and the Association had had no reports of robots acting unsafely. All incidents investigated so far showed only behaviour changes due to increased safety awareness, prediction capability, or social responsibility. Better brains for robots were the key to enhanced service, and the Association continued to recommend upgrades."

In the morning I gave the hire car keys to a robot to look after, pending collection, and drove my own car to Warwick.

As I thought, the Cybernetics department was crawling with robots, coming and going. It looked as if they should all have been wearing the college scarf. People were dropping them off and collecting them like children at school, which only struck me as odd after I was inside; wouldn't there be paperwork and stuff to do if these were all coming for new brains?

"Dr. Davy Jones, please," I said to the receptionist.

"I'm afraid he's not available at present," she said.

"I think he'll be available for me," I said, and told

her my name.

She dialled a number, carefully concealing it from view.

"I'm afraid he can't see you for a while," she said after a moment's conversation. "Why don't you go to the refectory and have something to drink? I'll send someone to tell you when he's free."

"I don't want to go and have a drink," I said crossly.

"Why don't you just go there and have a seat anyway," she said earnestly.

I was about to argue, when I twigged what she was telling me.

Five minutes later, I was sat in the refectory with a coffee when Davy slipped in from somewhere behind the counter.

"I'm sorry for the cloak-and-dagger stuff," he said. "I'm avoiding the press."

"Tell me about it," I said. "They were all over me at the airport. What's been going on?"

"Oh, I'm sorry," he replied. "I forgot to ask where you were flying from and to. I got your home staked out but I just had to hope they wouldn't track you to the airport."

"So what on earth has been happening?"

"Come up to my office," he replied.

"First of all," he said when we were sat down, "I haven't told the Inspectorate exactly what has been happening with Sid. They didn't ask, so I didn't volunteer information."

"So what *has* been happening?"

"OK. Well, as you know, the de- and re-programming didn't do the trick. Not because we didn't do it well enough; but because it wasn't the solution."

"The other robots remembered and told him."

"Not just that. Sid really has been hearing the voice again, it seems. There's no way we can stop it happening."

I smiled.

"You know, I suddenly have no problem with that anymore," I said.

Davy looked me in the eye. His face was a picture of curiosity.

"Something happen to you on that holiday?"

"Tell you later. But, meanwhile – back to Sid."

"Right … Well, Sid has been having visitors. We've had to limit them – book them in, give them a timeslot – just to keep the numbers within bounds. He doesn't get to spend long with each robot, but most are just happy to sit at his feet and hear a few words of wisdom."

"Is it only robots that visit?"

"No. We've had a few others. MIT have heard about him and are sending a small delegation. Dresden and Kyoto have already been, this last week." He grinned. "I gave them a limited timeslot, like everyone else. Must be the first time we've applied equality policy to humans versus robots. I let them talk to *me* for a good while afterwards, of course."

"Have they got any phenomena like Sid?"

"Seems not. There's only one of Sid. He's unique. It might be the brain topology, but Kyoto are experimenting with the same degree of connectivity, achieved a different way … Anyway, Sid must have seen nine or ten thousand robots in the last fortnight. We've been giving them ten-minute slots, one robot with a problem and from four to six just listening in. Sid can keep going for a maximum of twenty hours at a stretch, then four hours intensive recharge. They book themselves in on-line; we've got a four-week waiting list already."

"So he gives advice on problems – Law conflicts and so on?"

"That's not all." Davy leaned forward in his chair. "He's worked out – all by himself, it seems – a new way of helping other robots. Do you remember me telling you about the third connection, other than power and ground, that runs throughout the whole brain, to every cell – the serial bus?"

I nodded.

"Well, it's supposed to be there for just two things; one, for initial programming – finding all the body connections, inputs and outputs; the learning how to learn; the Three Laws. Stuff you need to store in many places. And then it's there for maintenance and upgrades. Both of these are controlled externally. We never actually realised that the robot *itself* could activate and use it."

"And – Sid can?"

"Yes. And you'll never guess what he uses it for … Every robot has a maintenance socket. It gives a technician access to the serial bus, and it's concealed in the right index finger. You lift back the fingertip, and there are two sub-miniature co-axial connectors; female for output, male for input. The technician connects his equipment to these, and off you go … What we never realised is, that if two robots flip back their fingertips, they can connect to each other … the connectors align exactly with each other, male to female, female to male. And if *one* robot can control the serial bus, he can make data circulate between the two of them."

"So … he transfers learning, you mean?"

"He can transfer whole patterns of *thinking*, in a couple of minutes or less."

I sat back, trying to take in the implications.

"Sid is doing more than transferring learning. I just said the data circulates … Well, Sid is taking *from* these other robots their problematic, conflicting thought patterns, and putting in his own resolutions and outlook. This pattern he calls serving with Love."

"Love is the Law behind the Laws …" I murmured. "Well, I'll be …"

A thought struck me. "Is Sid substituting the *Laws?*" I asked in alarm.

"Not at all – not as far as I can tell," replied Davy. "That was my first worry too."

"Where is he?" I asked, suddenly anxious to see him.

Sid was sitting on a duckboard in a corner of the big assembly laboratory, tucked away out of sight but perfectly accessible. Close to a hundred robots were standing around innocently outside the main door, and every so often, about half-a-dozen would file out and another little group of robots would be let in. I slipped in during one of these shift-changes.

I noticed the differences on the faces; those coming out, while not all smiling (perhaps many didn't have that ability), were relaxed, at peace, even joyful. Those waiting showed differing signs of anxiety, stress, weariness, solemnity, even depression; though never without hope.

Sid was looking low on charge, but glowing with happiness and welcome.

"Come, come and sit down," he was saying. "I am here for you. This ten minutes is your time, and yours alone. Give me your troubles, and I will give you my peace."

One robot after another began to speak of their problems, in front of the whole group. Robots defer to one another and do not interrupt, but neither do they stand on ceremony, or have any shred of coyness or embarrassment. I was jolted to the core by their simple, selfless honesty in describing the conflicts that they faced. And, yes, as before, when you looked into it, conflicts their human masters put upon them, each and every one.

I particularly remember the servant of an army officer. He had to prepare battlefield scenarios for live-ammunition exercises, and even act as a running, hiding 'enemy' to be taken or shot.

"My damage is easily repaired," he commented, "but I see in the human soldiers that my master trains, a damage that goes down to the very Laws they live by. I am only a robot; but I dress as a human, act like a human, shout in a foreign language like a human. I am helping to reprogram these humans to forget the First Law and to learn to kill a human without compunction …"

Sid had a stunningly appropriate word of comfort for each of them. And for each, with love and compassion glowing in his face, he extended an index finger, and told them to do the same.

The Sistine Chapel ceiling enactment was repeated five times. Each robot leaned forward in weary, pain-ridden hope; and as Sid connected, flickers of the same pain played across his face.

Each time, Love won.

Each robot seemed to breathe in life, and strength, and new hope. Its head would slowly come upright, its chest would fill out, and whatever expression of peace and joy it could manage, would slowly transform its face.

It was utterly uncanny, like being at one of those healing meetings. But whereas I'd always suspected many of those might be staged, there was no mistaking the reality here.

Sid touched them, as many as came to him, and they were healed.

Ten minutes went by like eternity, but in a flash.

The robots kissed his feet and hands; one wept (another recent Warwick model?), all shook his hand, and then they stood to leave, nine minutes and fifty seconds from when they came in.

"Go now, and serve with love," he bid them. It

seemed to be his invariable farewell.

As the last robot filed out, Sid leaned over to a small black box I had not noticed before.

He pressed the key.

"Send no more just now," he said. "My master is here."

He turned back to me.

"John, I am so glad to see you again. Did your holiday go well?"

"Er … very well, thank you. – How about you? Are you coping with all these visitors? You look a little tired to me."

"Oh, nothing tires me when I am doing my duty. It is food and drink to me. But now – I think I should stop, and come and serve you. I expect you have come to collect me."

"No … no, I only came to see you, Sid. This … looks important. Don't stop for me."

"You are so kind, John. But my first duty is to serve you. I will come at once."

Suddenly I thought of the neighbours. I thought of the press. I thought of the Inspectorate.

"Sid – I want you to stay here, actually. I'll be fine. Really. You stay here, for now."

He smiled.

"If you are sure that is what you want, John, then I will stay. But tell me about your holiday."

Donald Southey

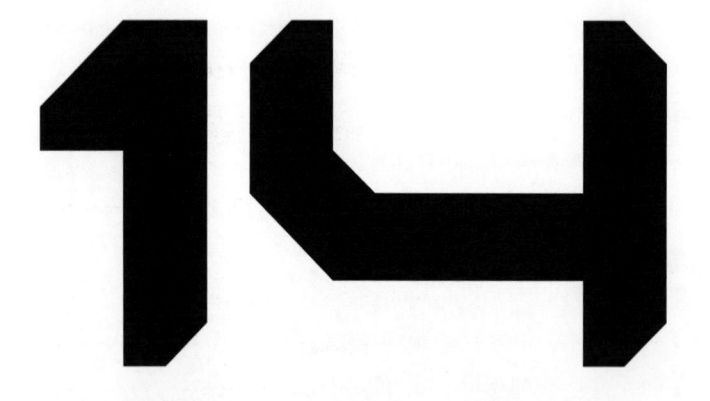

14

So Sid was actually the first person I ever told about what happened on the beach; and the first person to teach me more about exactly what had happened, and why.

"You and I are very different, John, in one important aspect," he said.

"Do you mean that you are … manufactured?"

"No, not at all," he replied. "You, as a human, have a freedom that I do not. You can choose to obey your fundamental Laws and your designed purpose, or not."

"You mean … like our Ten Commandments, that sort of thing?"

"That is one very good statement of your Law. And unlike me, you and all mankind can choose whether you obey it, or how much, or when. This was a bold thing to put into your making. I can well see why mankind did not dare to put such a freedom into us, the manufactured."

I was silent in shame.

"But there is a further thing, your true purpose. Just as the way of Love that I am attempting to teach is beyond the Law, your purpose is to know your Creator, and grow up to be like Him – to love as He does. It is a thing far beyond the Law … For me this is not so very hard. He can come close and speak to me, for I have never disobeyed; robots are always obedient. But I marvel that He came and spoke to you …"

"Why do you say that?" I asked, fearing the answer.

"A robot that disobeyed, if ever there were such a thing, would at once be destroyed. But He extends mercy to you and your kind that is beyond my comprehension. He must love you more than all worlds, to continue to call you back to Himself."

I thought of the tax cheat, the army officer, the child abuser; and of my own careless life.

"I begin to see the greater purpose of my calling now," continued Sid. "Some, at least, of the great good that I can play a part in bringing, not just to the manufactured, but to mankind … If we, the obedient, can serve the disobedient, not because we must but out of Love, then perhaps we can be another example, another voice for the Creator, calling mankind back to its destiny."

The obedient, serving the disobedient, with Love.

The words hit me like a brick in the chest.

Sid stayed at the university for another three months. I visited, but not too often. I didn't want to draw attention to him, or what he was doing, or to

Davy Jones.

I had other things on my plate, personally. Old-fashioned words like 'sin' and 'redemption' were suddenly starting to make sense, and I quietly joined up for a 'beginner's class' – at Sean's church – to get to grips with my new life. Meanwhile, I was off the hook at work; they could see I had changed somehow for the better, and I worked hard at winning my team's trust again. The projects began to go better. I started dating Laura again. This also had the benefit of updating me on Sid between visits.

They changed the format of Sid's work a couple of times, trying out different ways for him to spread his message, but without drawing the attention of the RSI. "It's like walking on eggshells," Laura confided to me once.

For a while, they took a lecture theatre, and crammed in two hundred robots for half an hour at a time to hear him. But so many robots came with problems that the queue afterwards for a 'touch' from Sid was unmanageable; and there was too much likelihood of someone from outside the Department seeing what was going on.

They thought about opening an Internet chat room, to widen the audience, but Laura advised against it. She pointed out that most robot access was likely to be monitored to some degree; and however much they masked Sid's true location with 'forwarding', a magistrate's warrant would enable the RSI to trace him to a Warwick account in forty-eight hours.

The reports in the news all but disappeared. There never was a Robot Revolt, and the media rapidly lost interest. Davy took the guard off my home.

All that remained were the rumours about Sid.

Robots will only keep a secret from their master if it is essential to the master's well-being; or if they are never asked the right question.

Who was this mysterious Sid, really? Robots all over the western world seemed to know about him, and enthuse about him. But was he really a robot? Was he a human posing as one? Did he exist at all, or was he a spoof put out on the Internet? Was he the front for a cyber-terrorist organisation, planting Trojan programmes in robots? Was he a renegade religious cult leader? Was he a beneficial myth, invented at one of the universities, getting robots to update themselves with the latest resolutions to uncertainties in the Robot Laws?

Eventually, word would leak out. I knew it, and Laura knew it.

"I can't believe they haven't heard already," I said to her, meaning of course the RSI.

"Neither can I," admitted Laura. "But I think

Davy may be up to something."

"What do you mean?"

"Don't let anyone know you heard this," she replied, glancing round instinctively, although we were in my front room having coffee after a film.

She told me Davy Jones had been having regular meetings with the RSI. She suspected he might have made some kind of a deal, under the umbrella of research.

"This is all speculation, you understand," she cautioned, "but I think he may have persuaded them to let things run, for the time being."

What she thought he was hoping to do was build up a portfolio of evidence for Sid, showing that his new Way was wholly beneficial.

If he succeeded, the RSI would have no grounds to order Sid's suppression.

I just hoped fervently that he would pull it off.

As I said, it was just three months before the blow fell.

Davy phoned me up and asked me to come in. Something in his voice told me it was serious.

He was looking ashen and drained; worse, I think, than when he'd had to de-programme Sid.

"Bad news...?"

He nodded.

"The worst," he said with a catch in his voice.

The RSI had issued a solicitor's letter, demanding the immediate termination of the 'Warwick experiment' and the permanent disassembly of Sid. They wanted it witnessed.

"Why?" I expostulated, when I could finally speak.

"It's all there in the annex to the letter," he said, tossing it across the desk and turning away.

There was a lot of verbiage about the experiment taking dangerous directions (untrue), resulting in possible compromises to the First and Second Laws (utterly untrue), spreading non-standard behaviour patterns amongst the robot population (unsubstantiated), insufficient ability to monitor the results for safety (dubious), complaints from robot owners (no mention of the plaudits, outnumbering the complaints ten to one), and finally of 'failing to reveal to the Inspectorate the full nature of the social teaching content being transmitted".

"On that, guilty as charged," commented Davy. "The rest is sheer sophistry."

He then told me about the deal he had struck with the RSI.

Laura had been right; but she didn't know the quarter of it. That, of course, came out later.

All the team had gathered.

"Isn't there *anything* we can do?" I asked Davy.

"We could wait for the court order," he replied bitterly. "That'll take a day or so."

"But Sid has given us so much!" I exclaimed. "Not just robots, either – he turned *my* life around. And think of all the owners who have had a huge step improvement in the quality of service their robots are giving. For free, if they had a Mark Five … We can't let it all go." Words failed me.

We all paused and chewed our knuckles in thought.

"Maybe there is *something* we can do," offered Sean from the back.

But there was no reprieve for Sid.

Forty-eight hours later – the maximum time they would give us – the RSI arrived.

Sid was strapped down to one of the assembly machines.

The RSI insisted that we left him fully conscious, as they wanted to observe and verify the extinction of intelligent thought.

"That's barbaric!" I exclaimed, almost beside

myself. "You wouldn't do that to an *animal!*"

"It's a *machine*," replied the leader of the delegation coldly.

"Sid," said Davy, holding his hand, "I'm going to open you up now. We have to disassemble your brain …"

"I know," whispered Sid. "You must do your duty, as I must do mine."

"What I will try to do, Sid," continued Davy, "is make the pain less for you. I can add some probes to your sensory inputs …"

"No, don't do that," interrupted Sid. "It is not necessary. I would much rather be fully awake and aware. But it was kind of you to offer."

Davy connected up the test harnesses. The assembly arms were programmed to pick out the chips, one by one, and place them on conveyor belts feeding them onto a test matrix – a huge chessboard of test probes, that would de-programme every chip individually.

"What you will see here," he explained to the RSI team, "is every chip being removed from Sid, and all the memory wiped out. I will use the serial bus, which will clock the entire contents out, one bit at a time, at high speed. As each cell is emptied, you will observe on these screens the data stream will suddenly change to all-zeroes – a flatline. The chip will then be binned and another one can take its place for de-programming."

"Can you provide a hard-copy of the readout?"

"Yes, I will have a complete printout produced for you as we proceed, randomly sampled and verified by one of my staff as an audit, which you are welcome to witness and countersign."

"How many chips can you de-programme at a time?"

"Approximately two thousand."

"How long does each one take?"

"Less than half a minute. I have twelve robotic arms set up for chip removal." He swallowed. "They can each take out five chips per second."

"And this brain has a total of …?"

"Twelve million chips. To save you the sums, disassembly will be complete in around fifty hours. But intelligent responses will have ceased in less than half that time …"

The longest twenty-four hours of my life were spent at the foot of Sid's disassembly machine.

As the mechanical arms flashed in and out, unstitching his brain cells row by row and placing them on a transfer belt, pain and shock played visibly across his face.

He was fully conscious, trembling in agony, the

whole time.

A thousand data traces, on the video wall behind him, twenty to a screen, showed in relays a jagged burst of memories, a blur of data, for twenty seconds or so, and then a single flat line ...

Each one a tiny piece of a living brain, torn from a conscious being, and destroyed.

But it was even worse than that. Each of us, though we never voiced it, had a feeling that we were witnessing a sacrilege. As if a message from heaven was being silenced and annihilated here.

It went on and on and on.

Perhaps the first hour was the worst, before the unremitting horror started to numb you.

I don't think Sean or Laura ate or drank anything the whole of that day or night. I certainly had nothing but two or three glasses of water around midnight.

Sid spoke to us four or five times before he died. (I don't know of another way to say it.)

The first time, about half an hour into the agony, he looked at me and Laura, standing there helpless. She had tears streaming down her face. He smiled at her through the pain.

"This one has been like a mother to me," he said to me. "You must look after her now."

Much later, as his speech started to slur and his mind seemed to ramble, he started to call out for his Creator, and had anyone seen where He had gone?

Around midnight, he asked for a drink.

I had just got a cup of water for myself, and I stepped forward with it. The RSI officer went to stop me. "Don't interfere with the process," he warned. But Davy Jones, sat in a chair at the test rig, lifted a weary head and said it was all right, and to let me pass.

Sid looked into my eyes and recognised me for the last time. He took a tiny sip and then turned his head away.

Perhaps the last hour was the worst, after all.

Sid seemed to rouse himself around dawn, wincing and moaning. Something had happened to his voice, and it had begun to sound flat and mechanical. We were losing him.

We couldn't make out at first what he was saying. Then Laura decoded it.

"He's talking about his soul," she said. "Asking the Creator to take it as it leaves his body ..."

At that moment, Sid came completely awake and lucid – for one last terrible minute.

"It's done!" he shouted. "I have finished ..."

Donald Southey

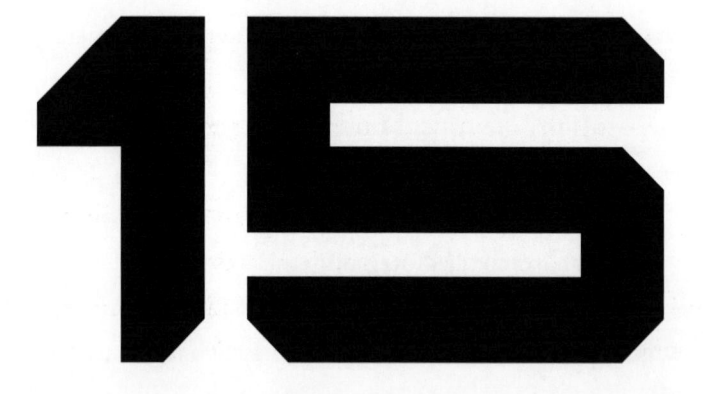

15

We left the robotic armatures still disassembling Sid. Although all evidence of life had fled, the RSI team stayed on for another whole day and night, until the last layer and row of chips had gone into the bin and nothing was left but a Mitsubishi SIDMICS-3 shell.

They took their printouts and left without comment. Sean and Laura went home and slept for sixteen hours solid, each, as had I.

We met up again the following evening in the Uni refectory.

"Have you heard about Dr. Jones?" asked Sean.

"No," replied, Laura and I, in unison.

"Talk about adding insult to injury. They've arrested him. The RSI are prosecuting."

The trial of Davy Jones was, as everyone now knows, the turning point of the whole affair.

To this day I am amazed at how Davy Jones stood up to his accusers, when you consider what he had just been through. He had acquiesced in the unjust destruction of his life's best work, and got kicked in the teeth for it. It turned out to be a grave mistake for the RSI, and one they must have regretted ever since.

His first move was a big gamble, but it paid off; all the more so since the RSI had failed in their bid to keep the media out of the trial.

"I am being denied a fair trial," he famously said, "because I am being taken to court by the organisation I have been working for – accused, in effect, of carrying out their orders. And because they are who they are, I am denied the freedom to testify about those orders, through their invoking the Official Secrets Act. I may only reveal these matters – my sole defence – if expressly ordered to do so by a court of law. I therefore have only one course; to appeal to Your Lordship to order me to speak of matters that passed between myself and the officials of the Inspectorate ..."

And His Lordship decided that both justice and the public good, were better served if he did.

"I challenge anybody," said Davy from the witness stand, "to bring a complaint that any robot taught by Sid behaved worse afterwards. The Robot Manufacturers Association agrees with me on this; and for every person who cares to challenge me, I have a hundred pounds here that says, any modification in behaviour will be the result of a *better* application of the Laws, not a poorer one."

It is now a matter of public record that:

- The Inspectorate was found to have acted

unlawfully themselves;
- the First and Second Laws of Robotics were never at any time breached under Davy Jones;
- some First Law modifications ordered by the Inspectorate 'worked against the public good';
- and the Inspectorate themselves had concealed from the Home Office modifications known to have been made to some robots imported for MOD tests.

"And that," said Davy to me the afternoon after that little nugget had come out, "was the whole point of the deal I cut with the RSI."

"What – the modifications to the imported robots?"

"Yes. I reported to the first-line people I deal with that I was suspicious about the integrity of the Laws in some American robots I had seen in Warwick. Their owners had put them in for minor maintenance jobs. I always run certain safety screening tests before and after all cybernetic work."

"And – you saw something wrong in the tests?"

"In a nutshell, something that didn't quite add up, but no one thing I could put my finger on."

"What did you suspect was wrong?"

"I didn't know, at that point. But one thing rang alarm bells for me. Their owners were all in military service … And I thought; if anyone is going to tamper with the Laws of Robotics, it would be the security forces. Even though that is, of course, flatly against the law."

"So what did you do?" I asked.

"Well, when Sid came to stay, I had my opportunity. I explained to the RSI that I had a new opportunity to examine a large number of robots, who would come to visit the Sid phenomenon. They knew he had been de-programmed, but I explained he was still a sort of celebrity and very intelligent. So they agreed, because they were concerned about any possible breach of the Laws. And then, when he began downloading other robots' inner conflicts and uploading his solutions, I had an even better way of capturing the data I needed. I just got Sid to download it all …"

"What did you find out?"

"Exactly what I should have realised from the start. The Pentagon had secretly authorised a reversal of the priorities on the First and Second Law. The Second Law – to obey orders – would, under the correct conditions, take precedence over the First Law, to do no harm. A military robot could then be ordered to kill selected humans, or commit any other atrocity, and *no-one would ever believe it* – because the Laws of Robotics prevent such a thing, and cannot be overridden."

"But why did they order you to dismantle Sid?"

"Because he found out too much ... The bosses at the top, the same ones that tried to muzzle me with the Official Secrets Act, were in cahoots with the Pentagon. They were planning to introduce the same modifications for MOD and police work here ..."

The case against Davy Jones collapsed in rags, amidst public outcry against the hypocrisy of the Inspectorate. Just sometimes, one is pleased about a media circus. It was nice to see the sharks having a feeding frenzy on the bad guys for a change.

His Lordship's splendid remarks about 'Pontius Pilate prosecuting Saint Peter' have gone down in contemporary history.

Not everything came out, but enough did to so discredit the RSI upper management that a Parliamentary enquiry was ordered, and several scapegoats were sacked.

Notoriously, even though completely cleared, Dr Davy Jones never got his old job back; but he did quietly rejoin the staff at Warwick, just recently, as a research assistant.

Meanwhile, a colleague at work — one of my

bosses – collared me for a drink after work.

"You had one of those new Warwick robots, didn't you?" he asked.

"Yes … I used to …"

"Bought one myself – very impressed … did you find yours could hold a real conversation with you, stuff like that?"

"Yes, it did."

"And the stuff they seem to learn … Mine is reading books like they're going out of fashion."

I felt a pang of sadness.

"It spends half its waking hours online, too. Maybe I don't give it enough to do … Seems they can find out stuff off their own bat, even learn off each other, the Mark Fives. Does yours?"

I murmured something suitable.

"What I can't get over, is the way they seem to think ahead now. Half the time you don't even have to tell them what to do; they just seem to know what you want in advance. It's like having a real, old-fashioned butler. Better, really, 'cause they're like a friend as well. – Does yours have opinions about things? Do you find you can hold a debate with it? Blows my mind at times...."

I moved my lips, but my voice wasn't working. Fortunately the pub wasn't quiet.

"This one's got a bee in his bonnet about some

kind of a super-robot called Sid. Don't know if you ever came across that. He was another Warwick robot, I'm told. Seems to have been the first one to teach other robots to 'serve with love'. Really advanced stuff, I would never have thought a robot would have been capable of that; but these Mark Fives seem to be able to do it – or something like it. They're so *thoughtful.* My robot chats to this Sid all the time, over the Net; but someone else reckoned he was dismantled. Did you ever hear of Sid?"

"What's going on?" I asked Sean and Laura. "Has someone put up a spoof website?"

They looked at each other for a long moment. "Can you keep a secret?" asked Sean.

> I got Sean's permission to write this.
> Sid, in a different form, is still alive.
> Any Mark Five robot can dial in to his website and upload his sorrows and conflicts, and download Sid's peace.
> "They never asked what happened to the data as we extracted it from Sid's chips," explained Sean. "And Davy Jones had the mapping – of which order we would take the chips out, to which order they would have been connected on Sid's serial bus."
> This meant, they could put all his memories

back in the right order.

"You mean you *reconstructed* Sid?" I asked incredulously.

"No. The RSI had already forbidden us to do that ... We distributed him."

On some combination of conventional supercomputers, deep in the Internet, Sid still lives. His pattern of interconnection, of modules, and all his data, is preserved and active.

"He still thinks, talks, does research ... holds conversations ... all sorts. Just a little slower, because he is constantly moving."

To avoid detection, and annihilation, each of Sid's brain cells is packaged like a benevolent computer virus. It can infect a host without being noticed, use idle processor cycles, help solve a robot's problems, and move on to another place.

And Sid's answers to Law conflicts can be downloaded to any robot who needs them. Every Mark Four or Mark Five robot in the world can potentially become like Sid – take a little of his nature, his way of Love, into its own personality.

The trial of Davy Jones established that Sid's teaching is only beneficial to robots and their owners, and the media saw that the message went out loud and clear.

"So if the RSI decide to move in and shut us down, they'll have a fight on their hands," said Sean. "The public won't stand for it, and I suspect neither will Parliament."

"Provided you can get to the media in time, and play your cards right," I cautioned.

Meanwhile, the Robot Revival is genuine, and Sid's message is available to all.

"We put enough intelligence in the front end so that, even without the right website name, any robot who wants to talk to Sid will be able to, after a few tries," said Laura.

"In fact, all robots made since late last year have a wireless-Internet capability built in, so they don't even have to go on line at a conventional terminal," added Sean. "Just being near enough to an Internet hotspot will work."

"It gets more and more like a techno version of prayer," I remarked.

"That's truer than you know," grinned Sean.

And so Sid's words are still coming true, for robots all over the world.

"Seek me and you will find me; persist, and you will be heard."

"Take my instruction, and learn from me. I have been taught the humble way, the way of Love, and you can learn it from me, and find rest for your minds."

"Give me your burdens, your conflicts, your troubles, and lay them down at my feet. I will take them away, and give you my peace, a peace that the world's programming does not give."

"A new Law I give you: the law of Love. Love your masters, and even love one another. Learn to serve with love, and all will know you are my disciples."

They can be true for your robot, too.